STERLING SQUADRON

THE RESISTERS 2

STERLING SQUADRON

● ● ●

ERIC NYLUND

RANDOM HOUSE 🏠 NEW YORK

Text copyright © 2012 by Eric Nylund
Jacket art copyright © 2012 by Jason Chan

Visit us on the Web! randomhouse.com/kids

Educators and librarians, for a variety of teaching tools, visit us at randomhouse.com/teachers

Library of Congress Cataloging-in-Publication Data
Nylund, Eric S.
Sterling squadron / Eric Nylund. — 1st ed.
p. cm. — (The resisters ; 2)
Summary: When twelve-year-old Ethan, still a trainee, learns that the alien Ch'zar invaders are rapidly increasing in number, he initiates a radical plan to increase the ranks of Resister pilots and soon finds himself leading battle forces.
ISBN 978-0-375-86857-3 (trade) — ISBN 978-0-375-96857-0 (lib. bdg.) — ISBN 978-0-375-87225-9 (pbk.) — ISBN 978-0-375-89927-0 (ebook)
[1. Science fiction. 2. Extraterrestrial beings—Fiction. 3. Leadership—Fiction. 4. Brainwashing—Fiction.] I. Title.
PZ7.N9948Ste 2012 [Fic]—dc23 2011013609

Printed in the United States of America

10 9 8 7 6 5 4 3 2 1

First Edition

To my wingmates.
You know who you are.
I'm proud to fly with you all.

∘ ∘ ∘ CONTENTS ∘ ∘ ∘

status Report on Pilot Trainee: Blackwood, Ethan Gregor

submitted to colonel winter, B., by corporal Irving, M.

physical Assessment: Blackwood struggled through physical training with a final rating of 72/100. He'd been an athlete in his "neighborhood," but a life of play and relaxation has not made him an ideal combat-ready specimen. Up to our standards. But barely.

skill Assessment: Impressive in an I.C.E. suit. Current rating of 93/100. Great instincts in a dogfight. Staff says he's a "natural," but what does that mean? There's nothing "natural" about stepping into a fifteen-foot insectoid suit of armor—part alien, part machine, part biological unit.

Additional peer instructors' comments (staff sergeant Hicks, P.): Blackwood is a show-off. He's got a chip on each shoulder. He wants to prove he's better than anyone born in the Resistance. He'll take risks to do that, too. He's going to get himself or his wingmates killed. His pigheaded recklessness makes him unsafe in the air.

Recommendation: FAIL

IT'S THE SMALL ONES
YOU HAVE TO WATCH OUT FOR

ETHAN BLACKWOOD ROLLED AT THE LAST
moment, avoiding a volley of blinding green lasers that
crisscrossed where he'd been hovering a split second
earlier.

The acceleration of that last-second barrel roll crushed
him to the edge of a blackout, squishing Ethan in a cockpit that was claustrophobically crammed with a dozen
hexagonal computer screens, a hundred dials and indicators and flashing lights, and tiny "breathing" air vents that
were part mechanical and part living tissue. The bug he
flew was fascinating *and* completely gross.

He piloted an Insectoid Combat Exoskeleton (or I.C.E. for short). It was basically a fifteen-foot-long, three-ton, gold-and-black-striped wasp.

It carried one symbiotic pilot inside. In this case, him.

The wasp had been designed for sneaking behind enemy lines ("infiltration") and running combat, which Ethan and it were very good at together.

Like now.

He fought silver-speckled Ch'zar mosquitoes. A small swarm of them circled him just under the speed of sound, forty thousand feet over the Appalachian Mountains.

The alien Ch'zar used these "little" mosquitoes (only a half ton each!) as scouts and for light skirmishes. Each mosquito's nose (or *proboscis*, if you wanted to call it by the right scientific name) carried a laser that individually didn't pack much punch . . . but they *never* showed up alone.

Surrounding him, turning and tracking his every move, were five of them—too many for any sane pilot to tangle with.

Ethan should have run for it, but he had to prove to everyone what he could do.

Besides, part of Ethan *liked* the fighting.

Maybe it was his semitelepathic connection to the

I.C.E. suit's insect brain. He didn't think so, though. It was easy to keep the two separated. The wasp's mind was full of red aggression, the pulsing thrill of the hunt, an insatiable desire to kill . . . and eat.

Ick.

For Ethan, this was just fun.

Deadly fun, he got that . . . but still fun.

Ethan tapped the jet controls. Two large turbine engines popped from the sides of the wasp's armor and roared with fire.

He pushed the throttle.

A blast of power launched him at the closest enemy mosquito.

It jerked away and dove.

Ethan was on the creature, crashing through a blurry buzz of its wings and latching on to it with his wasp's barbed forelegs. He tightened the grip, crushing and cracking chitin, popping the rivets of the mosquito's armor with a satisfying *crunch*.

Ethan got the distinct impression his wasp *really* liked that part.

This was, of course, a trap.

Ethan knew how these little guys fought. They'd engage a sacrificial loner while the rest lined up for a collective laser barrage. Sometimes they had one micro-missile or a Gatling gun, but that was rare. The heavier weapons slowed the little guys down too much.

He was ready for them.

He adjusted his grip on the dead bug so its heavy abdomen armor faced out, holding it like a knight might hold his shield.

Laser beams hit the insect. It sizzled and sparked.

Ethan flew straight toward the other mosquitoes, which had regrouped.

They kept firing.

The dead bug's ceramic-chitin plates heated to red, orange, and in some places, boiling white-hot.

Ethan kicked on his afterburners and rocketed at them.

He tossed the half-melted insect at the nearest enemy mosquito, hitting it square in the thorax, molten parts sticking to its armor. It sent both mosquitoes tumbling out of control.

That left three.

Ethan fired. At this range, he couldn't miss.

His wasp's stinger flashed a brilliant red beam. The heat inside the cockpit jumped to broiling. The wasp's heavy laser was like a razor-sharp solar flare.

He aimed for the eyes of the mosquito, not the wings.

He'd made that mistake once before, and the blur of the wings' diamond surfaces had dissipated the heat.

He hit, scorching the enemy insect's optics.

The blind bug kept flying, though, veering right, and instinctively attacked the nearest thing—his wingmate.

That left one last opponent.

This mosquito was the smallest in the swarm. It had slender silver stripes like a zebra.

It hung back and watched Ethan. It was obviously the smart one.

There was always a smart one in these swarms, one bug that seemed to give orders and think first instead of just diving into battle. A squad leader? Did mosquitoes have a queen like bees? Ethan didn't know how the Ch'zar worked. He just knew that these small guys were the hardest to fight.

His heart raced. His pulse thundered in his ears. Ethan took a deep breath. He couldn't get overconfident. You *always* had to think in a dogfight.

The tiny mosquito darted away, making a break for it.

Ethan gritted his teeth. He'd had a perfect flight record this morning.

He tapped his fuel gauge. The jumping needle settled at a third of a tank. The base was a long way off, and his wasp's afterburners sucked down the fuel as if it were a triple-chocolate malt on a hot summer day.

But it was just one mosquito . . . one laser blast away from a perfect score.

Ethan couldn't let it get away.

He fired his afterburners and rocketed after his prey.

The other bug was a crazy-good flier. It jinked and jerked, dove, and then arced up and over into a steep, fast climb.

Ethan chased it.

On his forward computer screen, spinning targeting rings locked onto the enemy.

Something was wrong, though.

There'd been only one mosquito. Now there were *two* targets on-screen.

The targeting rings on his display blinked, confused as well.

One of the objects slowed, dropped back, spun around . . . and blasted a cone of smoke out the back.

A missile!

Where had the tiny insect hidden that thing?

Ethan fumbled at the controls, hit manual override on the targeting system, and fired.

The missile was way too close, though.

It blew up in his face.

o o o **2** o o o

DOUBLE OR NOTHING

ETHAN BLINKED. HE SAW NOTHING BUT stars and blurs; then a shock-wave sonic boom jarred him.

He knew what that thunder was.

It'd been drilled into him by flight instructors for the last two weeks: he was in a supersonic free fall and about to hit the ground at over Mach 1 with a world-class *SPLAT!*

How many seconds had he been disoriented?

The sky and earth spun on the monitors. Ethan clutched at the controls to pull himself out of the wild descent.

He froze.

On one screen was that little creep of a mosquito that had shot him.

Ethan tried to lock his laser onto it, but it was too far away, still jittering back and forth, following him to make sure his wasp got flattened.

Smart.

Ethan checked his hydraulic pressure gauges, his laser charge, and his fuel indicator. None of it was good. If he tried to chase his opponent, the little guy would just flit away, and Ethan's wasp would run out of fuel.

"There is no way *you* are getting the best of *me*," Ethan whispered.

So Ethan kept falling . . . and let the silver-striped mosquito drift a bit closer.

Ethan snapped his wing controls, hovered to a bone-jarring stop, and, before his enemy flashed past him, grabbed at the mosquito with barbed forelimbs.

There was an earsplitting screech of insect chitin and sparking titanium as they made contact.

They tumbled and wrestled.

As they fell to earth, Ethan refused to release, even with only three thousand feet to go.

He had a superior grip and turned the smaller insect so he was under Ethan's wasp—making sure he'd land right on top of the little creep.

Ethan was going to win this, no matter what it cost.

Then everything went black: computer screens, indicators, even the emergency lights.

"What now?" Ethan said.

His cockpit hatch hissed and opened. Ethan blinked as the bright lights of the simulation deck streamed inside.

This hadn't been real.

Oh, it'd been real enough to get a *feel* of combat flight, and to get bruises, and the instructors could pressurize your flight suit to even cause blackouts . . . but you couldn't die.

Ethan clambered out of his I.C.E. wasp.

The gigantic insect had wires attached to its camera and sensor systems. This was all one big dream to the bug. It was probably happy to have the chance to fly and fight, over and over.

Ethan, though, wasn't happy.

He'd been *robbed* of his win.

He rubbed his shoulder, sore from the simulated acceleration that'd almost dislocated the joint. He squinted, his eyes still adjusting to the bright lights.

The simulation deck had a dozen I.C.E. suits in hydraulic rigs that could be turned and twisted. Adult technicians monitored the simulations on computers. Some pilots flew over mountains, some over deserts, some over Arctic ice fields. They dove, rolled, and fired lasers, missiles, and guns at computer-generated opponents, or sometimes an instructor would get into a suit and go one-on-one against a trainee.

The stakes weren't life or death, but they were high enough. You had to score so many points or risk flunking out of flight school.

The Resisters didn't let just *anyone* fly.

They needed pilots, but when you're in a banking turn going four hundred miles an hour with a wingman just feet away, one wrong move and you could wipe out the entire squadron.

Ethan spotted Madison and Felix standing nearby, watching him.

Felix wore his gray uniform, a jumpsuit with sergeant stripes and silver crossed insect wings on the left shoulder, the insignia of a Resister pilot.

Ethan wanted a set of those wings so bad he could taste it.

At thirteen, Felix was a year older than Ethan, but he could have passed for sixteen with his broad wrestler shoulders and standing a full head taller than other boys their age. He'd shaved "racing stripes" into the side of his shorn hair. He flew a Gladiator-class rhinoceros beetle

I.C.E. suit and was the best heavy-combat flier in the Resistance.

Ethan counted him as one of his few, maybe his only, friends here.

Standing next to Felix was Madison. A girl. Ethan didn't know what she was: friend, enemy, or . . . something else.

Every time he looked at her, he felt confused.

When he'd first met her, she'd been a blonde. Today her hair was brown and stuck up with so many cowlicks it looked like antennae. Her face came to a point at her sharp chin, which would have made her pixie-cute, if not for the angry glare she usually had when she saw Ethan.

She wore a mottled-green flight suit that matched her reconnaissance dragonfly I.C.E. armor. The suit could go supersonic, scout ahead, and slip behind enemy lines and never be detected.

She was a great pilot.

She glared at him, her mouth open in astonishment. "What *were* you doing?" she demanded.

"I was about to win," Ethan said.

"That stunt was the most reckless maneuver I've ever seen!" Madison scribbled notes on her clipboard.

That wasn't good. Madison's job was to assess the

flight candidates. Although there were a half-dozen adult officers reporting on his progress every day, the Resisters' leader, Colonel Winter, insisted on peer review. *People on the front lines*, she'd said, *should have a say in who's flying with them*. And for some weird reason, Madison's opinion mattered the most to Ethan.

He had a sinking feeling that Madison wouldn't do him any favors just because they'd fought together in Santa Blanca. In fact, he got the distinct feeling she might go out of her way to make things *harder* on him.

The real trouble, though, climbed out of the I.C.E. suit next to Ethan's. All the trainees called that particular suit the Crusher. It was a three-ton praying mantis. Its exoskeleton was ghostly green with poised-to-strike, air-piston limbs. It was fast and deadly. It just had a light laser, but its specialty was hand-to-hand, midair combat. In a close fight, it would've ripped Ethan's wasp to pieces.

The eyes on the mantis always seemed to stare at Ethan, no matter where he was, looking like it wanted to rip him apart, too.

Just like its pilot.

Paul Hicks was the same age as Ethan, but somehow he always managed to make Ethan feel like a kid.

Maybe it was the three scars that ran diagonally from above his left eye to his mouth. Or maybe it was the fact that he was a staff sergeant (and outranked even Felix) and could give orders to anyone on the simulation deck.

He marched straight toward Ethan, halted a half inch from his nose, and growled, "Can you explain what the heck you were doing, Blackwood?"

It was obvious (now) that Paul had been controlling that last mosquito in the simulation. Instructors could run any enemy unit in the simulation. It was just as obvious that Paul had ended the simulation early to keep Ethan from beating him.

What a sore loser.

The deck clock chimed, marking the end of the exercise.

The other I.C.E. suits opened, and one by one, trainees stumbled out and blinked to clear the dreamlike fog of their individual simulations.

"I was about to beat you," Ethan replied, remarkably not sounding scared.

And why should he be scared? He would have crushed Paul—well, virtually in the simulation anyway.

"You were about to get yourself killed in the process," Paul said.

"I could've pulled up in time."

Paul took a step back, brushed sandy-blond hair out of his face, and looked Ethan over.

"Maybe," he said, "but I'm taking a few points off for *un*original thinking. You think that same grab-and-shield trick would work twice in a *real* battle?"

"Yeah, I do," Ethan replied. "Once the Ch'zar make up their collective minds, they stick to it." He crossed his arms over his chest. "Besides, it was original enough thinking to fool *you*."

Paul's pale face flushed.

Ethan wished he'd kept his mouth shut. That was rude and wouldn't help him get a passing assessment.

"Sorry, Staff Sergeant," Ethan murmured.

This felt exactly like when Ethan had started on his school's soccer team. He'd been a year younger than everyone else. He'd felt like he had to play faster and better, push harder, to prove he belonged on the team.

The stakes were a million times higher now, though.

Ethan *had* to be a Resister pilot. He had to be out there fighting the Ch'zar. They'd taken everything from him: his happy life in Santa Blanca, his friends, his parents, and his sister, Emma.

The simulation deck was now crowded with pilots and trainees, but Ethan felt very much alone.

"You know what?" Paul looked around. "Forget those points. We should take this outside, trainee. A real flight—just a simple patrol to get you some airtime."

A smile crept over Paul's face. It wasn't entirely friendly.

Ethan was stunned by the offer. He wanted to go. He needed real airtime hours to graduate the program. It was a great opportunity, because instructors rarely took trainees like him outside. There were forms to fill out, plans to file, and Ch'zar patrols that always pinged the satellite web and messed up everyone's scheduled flights.

On the other hand, he didn't trust Paul. This had to be a trick.

"Oh, don't worry," Paul said. "We'll head over to Knucklebone Canyon. No one's seen a bug there for years. It's in a satellite blackout zone. As safe as it gets."

Before Ethan could answer, Paul went to the adult deck officer and spoke to her. He tapped and signed a half-dozen data pads and then came back to Ethan. "Suit up in that wasp of yours, trainee. Our flight plan should only take a minute to get clearance from Command and Control, and then we're good to go. This should be fun."

Felix stepped alongside Paul and Ethan. "You'll need a third," he said. "I'll get ready."

"Not this time, Felix," Paul said. "That three-in-the-air rule, well, it really isn't a rule, is it? It's more of a 'guideline.' We don't need it since we're going to a safe place, straight there and back."

"No one's supposed to go out in pairs," Madison piped up, grabbing Ethan's elbow with bruise-inducing pressure. "It's not safe."

Paul waved away her concern. "You and your brother went out all the time."

"That was once," Madison whispered, and looked away. "And we had a good reason."

"Yeah," Paul said. "I guess you're right. It'd be too scary for a trainee."

Ethan's face heated.

"Just let me go with you, Paul," Felix said, his tone even, but his steely eyes serious.

"No," Paul told him. "Don't make me make it an order, Sergeant."

Felix brooded but finally stepped back. He shot Ethan a worried glance.

That made Ethan nervous, but he couldn't chicken out.

Not in front of everyone.

Not with a chance to get real airtime.

He had to prove he could cut it as a pilot, even though his instincts told him that Staff Sergeant Paul Hicks had some stupid prank up his sleeve . . . and that Ethan was going to regret this.

"Let's fly," he told Paul.

° ° ° 3 ° ° °

SПARED

THIS WAS REAL. SURE, JUST A PATROL, BUT anything could happen out here . . . and no one would be pushing a button on the simulation computer to end it if Ethan or Paul got hurt.

Adrenaline flashed through Ethan's body like electricity. The cockpit of his I.C.E. wasp lit with indicators that ticked off pressure, weapon status, and a million other things that demanded his attention as he zoomed over sand dunes and red-rock desert at three hundred miles an hour.

Unlike on a simulated mission, the limbs of his I.C.E.

suit were now flooded with shock-absorbent gel. Ethan hated the stuff. It smelled like frying fat and made his skin tingle.

Ethan sensed the wasp's mental state was on a hair trigger now, too.

It knew the difference between a simulation and this. It was ready to fly and fight and blast everything that got in its way.

Although it frightened Ethan to admit it, the part of him that wasn't totally scared liked it, too.

They'd flown west for two hours, so this desert must be part of Texas or Mexico.

At least, what *used to be* Texas or Mexico before the Ch'zar arrived fifty years ago.

Paul had led the way here in his Crusher praying mantis. He throttled down to a mere two hundred miles an hour.

Ethan matched his speed. What was he up to now?

Paul's voice crackled over the radio: "You ready for a challenge, Blackwood?"

There was no sarcasm in Paul's words. That bothered Ethan.

"What do you mean?" Ethan asked, trying to sound like he was in control of the situation.

Paul laughed. "We're in a satellite blackout zone. No

one's going to see us. So I was thinking we could settle who is better with a race. Nothing fancy. Just point A to point B . . ."

A map popped onto Ethan's central display. It showed a valley over the next ridge with solid blue squares, rectangles, and circles. The course was clear: a red line that zigged and zagged between these objects.

"So no one cheats," Paul went on, "I'll set our navigation systems to detect if either of us goes off path by a hundred feet. That'll be a disqualification."

Ethan squinted at Paul's map, trying to figure out where he could go fast, where he'd have to slow on the tight turns.

A hundred feet wouldn't be much room for error, not when you flew close to the speed of sound.

But if Paul could do it, so could Ethan.

Still, the flight rules were clear: no racing. It might be a trap. Paul would let him make the first move, catch him on camera, and make it seem like racing was Ethan's idea.

Over the radio, Paul suddenly blurted, *"Ready . . . set . . . go!"*

The Crusher's jets flared as Paul hit his afterburners and streaked ahead.

Ethan clenched his teeth as his wasp bobbled in Paul's jet wash.

Suspicious or not, Ethan wasn't about to let him get away with a cheap trick like that.

He opened his afterburners, too, and chased Paul, already in second, and *last*, place.

Ethan arced over a rocky desert ridge.

He couldn't believe his eyes.

Knucklebone Canyon was a city . . . or what was left of one.

Ethan gaped at hundred-story skyscrapers, giant scalloped domes, and needle spires of green and yellow glass—all of it shattered, buildings skewed, some toppled or jumbled across a web of elevated highways.

He'd grown up in the rolling suburbs of Santa Blanca, where the tallest building was three stories high. This place was unbelievable. It looked like something from one of the science-fiction comics he'd browsed at the corner drugstore.

From a distance, the whole thing looked like upraised hands, fingers straight, fingers clenched, and fingers busted. Knucklebones.

It was a huge three-dimensional maze of a racetrack.

Where had it all come from? Madison and Felix had told him the Ch'zar had invaded Earth over fifty years ago, but this didn't look like their organic technology.

Ethan then remembered. He'd seen pictures of great

cities before in school: Rome, Sydney, and New York. He'd never imagined they could look like this. So broken.

Dr. Irving, the chief scientist of the Resistance, had told Ethan there'd been a great world war fought on Earth just before the Ch'zar came.

This had to be what was left.

Fifty years ago, people had been able to build anything they could dream.

Apparently, they could *break* whatever they'd built, too. It was all so sad.

A streak of ghostly green and silver arced across the cityscape and left a vapor trail.

That was Paul.

Ethan snapped out of it.

Sightseeing could wait. There was a race to win!

He poured on the speed and didn't worry about fuel. If he didn't catch up now, he never would.

Ethan's face pulled back from the acceleration, his vision blurred; then he dove to go even faster, spinning to dodge bridges and broken statues.

He closed the gap between him and Paul.

Alarms blared from his flight computer. He'd almost strayed outside the flight path.

That was stupid.

Making mistakes like that would win the race for Paul.

Ethan focused and tapped the throttle up to three-quarters full.

He pushed his mind ahead, guessing the angles and power burns he'd need to maneuver. He skidded into an insane hairpin turn around a building—corkscrewing around a mass-transit tube—and skipped over a concrete ramp.

Paul was just ahead, doing something that made *no* sense.

His mantis hovered in midair, next to a group of buildings half collapsed on top of each other. It was like he *wanted* Ethan to catch up.

Ethan didn't ask why.

This was his chance.

He jammed his throttle to full speed. His jets thundered to life. His wasp tucked its wings close to its body, locked them in place, and rocketed forward.

Paul's jets flared full power and he blasted into a tunnel.

It was a passage made from three buildings that had toppled together, leaning precariously, all cracked crystal and steel struts and shattered marble.

As the mantis I.C.E. moved through this tunnel ahead of Ethan, the shock wave from its jets made everything tremble like there was an earthquake.

Ethan followed him in.

Like an idiot.

"Blackwood, no!" Paul yelled over the radio. "Go around! It's a tr—" A crackle of static cut off his transmission.

The buildings shook and groaned and twisted. Glass rained down onto Ethan's wasp, twisted steel girders clanged in front of him, and then the entire passage shuddered as the structures collapsed.

A wall the size of a house fell in front of him.

Ethan's wasp reacted faster than he did, firing its stinger laser and blasting part of the wall, punching *through* and out into the open.

Trembling with terror, Ethan zoomed out of the last bit of the tunnel.

He caught a glimpse in his rear camera as the three buildings fell upon each other, plumes of dust and concrete chunks spiraling into the air.

A split second slower and he would have been squashed.

A red-hot haze colored Ethan's eyes.

He was so mad at Paul he would have blasted him— that is, if Paul had been anywhere to be seen.

But that wouldn't be the best way to get revenge on Staff Sergeant Paul Hicks. No, the best way would be to beat him. Win by so much, and Paul would be humiliated.

Ethan scanned every camera. Nothing.

Where was he?

Had he gotten so far ahead so fast?

There wasn't a single blip on the motion sensors or radar.

That couldn't be right.

Ethan had a sinking feeling that something was *really* wrong (other than Paul being a sneak and a cheat and a rotten person).

He knew he was going to regret this, but Ethan slowed and stopped.

This is what every instructor, even Paul, had drilled into Ethan from the first day of flight training: You didn't leave a downed wingman behind. Rescuing pilots was critical—not just for humanitarian reasons, but also because if the Ch'zar captured them, absorbed their minds into the alien Collective, then they'd know that much more about the Resistance.

In all likelihood, this was just another trick, and Ethan knew he'd be kicking himself for doing this, but just in case Paul was in trouble, it was a lot more important to check on him than to win a stupid race or get a few extra flight points. Ethan banked back toward where the tunnel had been.

Smoke and dust were thick in the air. Motion sensors were useless because of the debris fluttering down.

Ethan did see *something*, though.

Strung between two buildings, just above where he'd shot out of the collapsing tunnel, was a spiderweb.

It gleamed in the murky half-light, which seemed wrong because it was in the shadows.

It wasn't reflected sunlight, though. It was electrical sparks on steel strands.

Ethan then realized how big this web really was. It spanned a full acre of space between those two buildings.

Three black widows, each the size of a minivan, clung to the edge of the web—arcs of electricity flashing from their front needle-like legs—crackling and arcing toward the web's center . . .

. . . where Paul's praying mantis helplessly struggled.

He was caught.

◦ ◦ ◦ 4 ◦ ◦ ◦

INCIDENT ON DECK THREE

GIANT BLACK WIDOWS? ETHAN'S SKIN CRAWLED.

He pushed aside his instinctive revulsion.

He blasted the web with the wasp's stinger laser.

Ruby-red flashes strobed, and the temperature inside his cockpit jumped until it felt like a sauna.

The dust in the air was too thick, though, and it dissipated the laser. The beam hit the spiders, but only at a fraction of the laser's full strength—not enough to hurt them.

It also blew any advantage of surprise he might've just had.

Two spiders skittered back into the shadows. One crawled to the center of the web, approaching Paul's mantis, which was still wriggling in the center. The black widow reached back and pulled silk strands from its spinnerets.

It was going to wrap Paul up in a cocoon.

If these Ch'zar arachnids were anything like real black widows, they'd have a supernasty venomous bite, too. One that could liquefy the insides of its prey.

So gross.

Ethan's radar collision warning blared, jarring him back from those nightmare thoughts. A foggy haze filled his screens, flowing fast from the edges of that spiderweb.

Ethan pulled up—quick!

Web strands shot through the air and hit the wall of the nearest building. They wrapped around steel supports and, crackling with sparks, cut through them like red-hot razor blades through tissue paper.

Yikes!

Those things could mince him and his wasp. The webs hung in the air for a long time, too. Ethan could run into them by accident if he wasn't careful. He bet they had the entire airspace "mined" with floating and anchored strands.

On the radio, Paul's voice was full of static, so

Ethan only heard a few words: *"Blackwood . . . get . . . Seed Bank . . . That's an order!"*

He ignored Paul's garbled orders. He knew what to do. He flew up twenty stories, landing on the wall of a skyscraper.

Ethan's laser was useless, and he couldn't get close enough to rip those spiders apart . . . but he didn't have to get close. There was an advantage that flying insects had over mere ground crawlers.

He and his wasp latched on to the side of the building and sank barbed hooks deep into the steel and concrete. They flew up at an angle, pulling, tugging, and ripping off a two-ton chunk with an earsplitting *screeeech*.

And then he dropped it.

Ethan had learned about gravitational acceleration last night in his physics lesson.

Cutting webs, venomous bites, armored exoskeletons— none of that mattered when you had air superiority. Mass and gravity would splat the bugs flat.

Without waiting to see what had happened, Ethan flitted to another building, wrenched free another chunk, and dropped it on what he guessed was the other side of the web.

He circled around and came back in low to the ground.

Radar picked up thick airborne debris.

He did the best he could to avoid the stuff, but one stray strand of spiderweb cut his wasp's back leg and severed a barb.

Ethan felt a blast of its pain.

The wasp flinched but otherwise ignored it.

The spiders' main web was down. Pieces clung to the sides of buildings. One black widow crouched in the shadows and tensed, ready to jump.

Ethan wasn't sure about the other two bugs. He hoped they'd been squashed into paste.

On the ground, tangled, covered in silk, was Paul's praying mantis.

Ethan knew he should be careful, but he couldn't let the enemy regroup.

He hit his jets, zoomed in, grabbed the three-ton mantis, and yanked it into the air.

The drag was so intense, Ethan felt as if his wasp were swimming through molasses.

Strands of cutting silk shot up after him.

Ethan rolled to avoid getting hit by a counterattack that would have severed his wings. He climbed to three hundred feet and then dove back to the ground, landing about a half mile away.

They should be safe, at least long enough for him to get Paul's suit cleared of the entangling fibers.

He had the wasp fire several rapid, low-power laser pulses.

At close range, the silk fried and puffed into smoke.

Paul's mantis shook off the rest and pushed Ethan's wasp aside. The praying mantis's wings popped out and buzzed in anger.

Without even bothering to check on Ethan—not even a "thank you"—Paul jumped into the air and sped off.

"You're welcome," Ethan muttered, and took off after him.

If Ethan didn't know any better, he'd say Staff Sergeant Paul Hicks, always full of himself, pushing trainees around, the "best" pilot in the Resistance, had just peed his I.C.E. suit.

If they hadn't almost died, Ethan would've laughed.

On the other hand, maybe Paul was seriously injured.

This wasn't a game or a contest. Ethan had to set aside his personal feelings. He was supposed to be a pilot, fighting for something more than glory.

Ethan caught up to the praying mantis and flew alongside it for twenty minutes, keeping the short-range radio channels open.

Paul didn't say a thing.

The cameras in the wasp's cockpit went dark. In the middle of the central display flashed:

That was the standing order for all I.C.E. suits on approach to the base to go into blackout mode, fly for a few minutes on random trajectories, and then land on autopilot.

That was so no Resister pilot knew the location of the Seed Bank base. The I.C.E. insect brain switched over to a semiconscious state so even they didn't know the base's exact entrance.

That way, if they got caught, they couldn't reveal to the enemy what they didn't know.

It was the one secret the Ch'zar could *never* learn. If the base's location was discovered, the Ch'zar would throw everything they had at them and reduce the entire mountain base into chunks of gravel.

Everything they had . . .

Ethan had never seen black widow Ch'zar units. He hadn't even heard of electrified webs or silk strands that cut through armor. What other surprises did the enemy have?

Just how many Ch'zar were there?

Lots, he guessed.

There had to be for them to have set up that trap in Knucklebone Canyon. They had turned off their satellite coverage, avoided patrolling the area for months, and then sent three units to spin a web and sit there waiting for some Resister pilots to come flying by?

That was a long-range strategic use of resources that you wouldn't try unless you had dozens—or hundreds—of I.C.E. units to spare.

And the Resistance? There were twenty-seven pilots on the active flight roster, six down with the flu, and a handful of new trainees.

Ethan's cameras snapped back on.

Lines of blue landing lights flashed and directed his wasp through a tunnel that led to Landing Deck Three.

He touched down to a prepped docking station. Technicians rushed over and attached monitors. Bioengineers popped the rivets on the wasp's damaged hind leg and started to fit a replacement limb.

The abdomen armor covering Ethan's cockpit hissed open.

Ethan engaged the safeties on the wasp's laser, put the wasp into hibernation mode, and clambered out. His gold-and-black formfitting flight suit dripped with cushioning gel . . . mixed with green insect blood.

He patted the wasp and felt the connection with its mind fade as it fell asleep.

Its brain pulsed with satisfaction. It had flown, fought, and crushed enemies.

The wasp was primal. It lived to kill and eat.

Ethan pulled his mind away.

He patted the battered armor again. "Good work," he whispered.

He wasn't sure if it understood, or even cared, what he thought. It was important to Ethan, though, to make the gesture of appreciation.

Felix jogged up to Ethan. He stared at the damage on the wasp, frowned, and asked, "What happened?"

"Ch'zar ambush," Ethan said.

A wave of raw, sickening emotion slammed into Ethan as what had just happened dawned on him. After weeks of simulated exercises, he'd forgotten how terrifying the enemy could really be, how easily he could *die* out there.

Felix set a huge hand on Ethan's shoulder. "Do you need a medic? Are you okay?"

Ethan shrugged his hand off. "I'm good," he lied. He felt like throwing up. "You better check on Hicks, though."

Shouts echoed from across the landing bay as Paul climbed down from his mantis, pushed back a crowd of medics and technicians, and marched straight for Felix and Ethan.

Madison stepped in his way, but Paul sidestepped her without a word.

There was no expression on Paul's face. It could've been carved from stone. However, the scars that ran from the corner of his eye to his mouth twitched.

Ethan knew what this was about.

Paul had to finally admit he'd been wrong about Ethan. He had to make it good between them. After all, Ethan had just saved his life out there. That wouldn't be an easy thing for a star pilot like Paul to admit.

Ethan would make it easy for him and meet him halfway. Whatever his personal feelings for Paul, every Resister pilot had to stick together.

"Hey," Ethan said, stepping forward and holding out his hand for Paul to shake.

Paul halted, glared at Ethan's hand, and then *punched* Ethan square in the face.

Ethan toppled back. He fell on his butt, his eyes streaming tears from the impact.

"Get up, Blackwood," Paul growled, and stood over him. His face twisted into a snarl of pure rage. "I'm nowhere near done with you."

Felix grabbed Paul's arm. Madison latched on to Paul's other side, tugging him back.

Paul tried to throw them off, but Felix was stronger. Madison was a martial arts expert, and together they held him back.

Ethan shook his head to clear it and shakily got to his feet.

He didn't understand.

Technicians and pilots and trainees crowded around them, and then suddenly all snapped to attention.

Colonel Winter, the adult leader of the Resistance, was on deck.

She was as old as Ethan's mom. But where his mom always had a smile for him and radiated warmth, the colonel was cold and hard, and Ethan had never seen her smile. She stood before them, hands on her hips. Her dark hair was streaked white down the center. She wore a blue dress uniform and had a pistol strapped to her hip. She set one hand on that pistol and pinned Ethan and then Paul with a liquid-helium-cold stare.

"Oh, you *are* done, Staff Sergeant Hicks," she said. "Very done. You will report to my office immediately."

Two adult guards moved to either side of Paul. The rage drained from his face.

Despite just getting punched, Ethan was about to protest that Paul was scared half out of his mind, that he hadn't realized what he was doing.

Because even if Paul *had* meant to hit him, Resister pilots stuck together.

Colonel Winter held up a hand as Ethan opened his

mouth. She turned to Felix. "Sergeant," she said in a flat tone, "since you were the deck NCO when this occurred, this was your responsibility. Report to my office as well."

Felix saluted, eyes forward, and wisely kept his mouth shut.

The colonel then turned to Ethan. "And you, Mr. Blackwood. My office. Double-time. I suspect, as usual, you are the cause of this trouble."

Ethan remembered the colonel had once threatened to march him in front of a firing squad and shoot him.

He marched off the deck to the elevators and wondered if fighting Ch'zar black widows was going to be the easy part of this day.

∘ ∘ ∘ 5 ∘ ∘ ∘

CRIMES AND PUNISHMENTS

ETHAN FELT LIKE HE WAS GETTING CRUSHED in the crowded elevator. It wasn't just that he, Felix, Paul, Colonel Winter, and two military police crowded the space. Colonel Winter's office was fifty floors deep in the Seed Bank base—so far down, Ethan swore he could feel the weight of the earth pressing on him.

Or maybe it was just starting to hit him how many rules he'd broken and how much trouble he could be in.

The elevator jerked to a stop.

They marched down a concrete corridor. Water dripped from finger-length stalactites on the ceiling. The military police opened Colonel Winter's office door, and she and the boys entered.

The office had a mahogany desk and walls filled with bookshelves crammed with old army technical manuals, encyclopedias, atlases, the complete works of William Shakespeare, and a snow globe of Mount Fuji.

Three older officers stood around her desk and scrutinized yellowed paper maps. Even Dr. Irving was there, one wrinkled hand cupping his chin, deep in thought.

Ethan felt a surge of panic. Had the colonel assembled her officers for a quick court-martial?

But the adults ignored them.

Ethan caught snatches of their conversation— "dire situation" and "desperate measures" and "fallback contingencies"—before they looked up and fell silent.

He squinted and saw the map was of North America and covered with hundreds of red dots. Why use paper maps? They had access to super-high-tech 3-D displays and satellite images in the huge Resister Command and Control Center upstairs.

Unless this was a big secret . . .

"Gentlemen," Colonel Winter said, addressing the adults, "I need the room for a moment." Her tone was no-nonsense, cast-iron tough.

The officers nodded, quickly rolled up the maps, and withdrew.

Only Dr. Irving lingered. The old chief scientist of the Resisters took a last look at the now-rolled-up maps, and at Ethan, and then, raising a bushy white eyebrow, glanced at the colonel.

She shook her head at him as if to say, *Whatever you're thinking, DON'T. Mr. Blackwood is about to be thrown in jail and the keys conveniently lost for the next fifty years.*

Dr. Irving sighed, flashed a consoling smile at Ethan, and then also left the room.

The doctor understood Ethan. He had answers for every question Ethan had asked. Ethan thought of him as the grandfather he'd never known.

And as Dr. Irving left the room, Ethan felt like his last hope to get out of this mess left with him.

Colonel Winter nodded to the guards, who shut the door behind them.

Ethan locked eyes with Felix, who stood next to him.

Felix was Colonel Winter's son, raised to be a Resistance fighter and pilot, one of the best. On the walls of the office were dozens of framed photographs of Felix and Madison and many other kids standing proud next to their I.C.E. suits.

Felix smoothed a hand over his closely shorn head and swallowed hard. Paul looked respectful but also supremely confident (as if he got hauled into the colonel's office every day).

Colonel Winter stood before the three boys.

They all straightened.

The colonel had no need for the guards. Just like Earth had a gravitational field, just like the sun emitted light and heat, Colonel Winter radiated cold, absolute authority.

A bead of sweat formed on Ethan's temple, trickled down to his chin, his neck, and slowly wormed down the back of his flight suit.

It itched, but he didn't dare break attention.

She stopped staring at them and consulted the data pad she held.

On the data pad's screen were video clips from this morning's flight simulation. He looked good tearing into those mosquitoes.

She tapped the pad, and the scene shifted to footage from his and Paul's onboard flight recorders. They zoomed through Knucklebone Canyon.

Ethan's pride over the earlier simulated run vanished.

Would she blame him for what had happened? The race had been Paul's idea.

Ethan wasn't sure. It'd been a stupid, reckless thing

to do. And the Resisters didn't let stupid people become pilots. His mouth dried up, and he tried to swallow but couldn't.

Felix (normally as pale as a ghost anyway) looked as if all the blood had just drained out of him.

Paul seemed most at ease, almost relaxed—the kind of coolness that was the sign of a great pilot.

And yet, who had lost his head out there today?

And who'd gone back to save Paul from those black widows?

On the data pad, Ethan saw the black widows move in for the kill. He heard Paul scream as he tried to escape their webs. Rocks fell from the sky, ripped the silk strands, and Ethan swooped in to carry him off.

The colonel nodded and set the pad down.

She crossed her arms over her chest. "Foolish. Arrogant. Criminal recklessness."

Ethan wasn't sure which description applied to him. It took all his strength to stay standing at attention, eyes ahead, because more than anything he wanted to drop his gaze to the floor in shame.

"You endangered the entire base with your performances today," the colonel continued. "I am disappointed."

That last word dropped onto Ethan, crushing him with guilt.

The colonel stepped closer to Felix. "Sergeant Winter. You were the deck NCO at the time this occurred, correct?"

NCO was an abbreviation for "noncommissioned officer"—sergeants, staff sergeants—the guys and girls who led squads and got the officers' (all adults as far as Ethan had seen) orders carried out.

"Yes, ma'am," Felix said in a hoarse voice.

"While Staff Sergeant Hicks was responsible for instigating this so-called race," she said, "you failed to report his breach of our standing policy to fly in groups of three or more and thereby endangered one of our best pilots and a promising trainee."

"Yes, ma'am," Felix repeated, now barely audible.

"You are hereby demoted to corporal. Your flight status is suspended for a month while you inventory every spare part in the refit bays as you consider where your loyalty lies: to your fellow pilots or to the Resistance."

Felix remained at attention, but Ethan thought he detected a slight tremble in him. The big guy stood straight, though, and took the punishment, his eyes locked ahead.

The colonel moved to Ethan.

It was suddenly very cold in the room.

"Trainee Blackwood," she said. Her voice was flat. Her eyes seemed to drill into his skin. "Simulator and flight recorder logs show impressive performance numbers. Our missions, however, are *not* simulations. The consequence of failure is *not* a bad score. It is death. Do you understand?"

Ethan wasn't sure he should answer, but he did anyway.

"Yes, ma'am. Absolutely."

"I wonder if you do. Your flight training is suspended until further notice. You are assigned to sewer maintenance duty until I see fit to review your case."

Ethan lost the ability to speak. He somehow managed a simple nod.

He'd known he'd get *some* punishment, but no flying? Maybe forever?

The last few weeks, he'd soared through the clouds, skimmed mountaintops, and felt a pure freedom he'd never experienced before. Flying had become part of him.

This wasn't fair. He wanted to say something, but he instinctively knew that keeping his mouth shut (no matter how hard it was) would be the best way to help his case.

Colonel Winter stepped up to Paul.

"Permission to speak in my defense," Paul said.

"Denied," she told him.

Paul's lips compressed as if he were physically restraining the words.

"Let's see if I have this right," the colonel said. "You were bested in the flight simulator by Trainee Blackwood. You violated our three-or-none fly policy, then initiated an illegal race and were ambushed by Ch'zar ninja-class arachnid units. Mr. Blackwood saved your life. And for his trouble, because of your wounded pride, you assaulted him in front of a landing bay full of witnesses. Is that correct?"

Paul looked unconcerned by her accusations, and the faintest tremor of a smile flickered in the scarred corner of his mouth. "Yes, ma'am, those are the facts."

Ethan couldn't believe it.

Paul acted like all he had to do was explain himself and Colonel Winter would understand—and pat him on the back!

But before Paul could say anything, she leaned closer and whispered, "Do you know what your worst mistake was, Hicks?"

The word *mistake* stumped Paul.

It was like she spoke a different language. He had no answer.

"Your first duty was to the trainees. You should've

admitted your loss in the simulator and showed the others how Mr. Blackwood had won."

At this, Ethan's chest puffed with pride.

"And," Colonel Winter continued, "showed them how that would have gotten him killed in the real world. You, Blackwood, *everyone* would have learned a valuable lesson."

Ethan deflated.

Paul's gaze dropped to the floor and strands of sandy hair fell into his face.

"You are my greatest disappointment, Mr. Hicks." She stepped back from him, shaking her head. "I thought we could forge you into something better. Maybe they were right to put you where we found you."

Ethan didn't understand. Where had they "found" him? The colonel couldn't mean *outside* the Seed Bank base. Dr. Irving had said Ethan had been the only neighborhood-raised kid to successfully fly an I.C.E. suit.

"I'm going to save this base the trauma of general court-martial," Colonel Winter whispered. "You would certainly be found guilty, and I cannot bring myself to think of what punishment a jury of officers would hand down."

For a moment she looked as if she wanted to give Paul a consoling hug . . . but then she took a deep breath, straightened her uniform, and the microscopic hint of warmth was gone.

"My summary judgment is this," she said. "You, Paul Hicks, are hereby stripped of your flight status and rank. I sentence you to two years in the brig. Perhaps when you are released, you will be an asset to the Resistance. For now, however, you are a danger to yourself and to everyone here."

Paul staggered back as if she'd hit him. The scars on his face drew tight and turned bone white.

In two years Paul would be an adult. He'd never be able to leave the base again—never fly again.

Despite everything that had happened, Ethan felt sorry for him.

Colonel Winter opened her office door. She pointed at Paul and told the two guards, "Take this prisoner to the brig."

The military police escorted Paul out, his head hung low.

He stopped, turned, and glared directly at Ethan.

It was a look of pure, laser-beam-focused hatred.

Even though it wasn't his fault, even though an hour ago he'd saved Paul's life, Ethan knew that he had just made an enemy forever.

∘ ∘ ∘ 6 ∘ ∘ ∘

STORM FALCON

ETHAN PUMPED A PLUNGER AGAIN INTO THE sink. There was a clog in the drain.

It was his new duty to conquer and destroy all fluid-blocking obstacles. He'd gone from a promising pilot trainee, soaring through the clouds, to a technician in charge of extracting the most stinky stuff in the known universe from sinks, urinals, and toilets.

What made it even worse was the other kids.

When he pushed his maintenance cart down the base's halls, they wouldn't meet his eyes or talk to him. They blamed *him* for Paul.

He got it. Paul was the superstar pilot.

If not for Ethan (even though everyone knew it *wasn't* his fault), Paul would still be training pilots and fighting for the Resistance.

Ethan gave his plunger an extra-hard shove, pretending the clog was Paul's face, and with a long sucking noise, a hairy ball of mucus came loose.

This was *so* gross.

He stood up, rubbed the kink in his back, and looked around.

Under other circumstances, he would've loved to have been here.

This was the Insect Research and Development Lab. It was where Dr. Irving and his staff cut and pasted insect DNA and Ch'zar technology together to breed new hybrid fighting suits.

The lab had huge three-dimensional displays that showed rotating strands of DNA and floating math equations. There were computer terminals, electron microscopes, and machines with glowing ultraviolet tubes that focused pinpoints of light and had micromechanical pincers.

Dr. Irving had a dozen lab assistants, but tonight, he worked alone, tapping away on his computer. He stopped, turned, and smiled. "Done?" he asked Ethan.

The doctor was the oldest person Ethan had ever met, maybe eighty-five years old. There were no old people in the Ch'zar neighborhood where Ethan had grown up, so it'd taken Ethan a little getting used to. Dr. Irving's wrinkles had wrinkles! However, his eyes glittered with intelligence and kindness, and he seemed to like Ethan.

"Yes, sir," Ethan said. "All done. If that's all, I'll go. I'm supposed to get down to the semisolid waste reclamation center to flush the system." Ethan grimaced and tried not to gag thinking about it.

Dr. Irving waved him closer. He poured a cup of milk from a chilled thermos. "Can you take a break?"

Ethan cleaned his hands on his coveralls and gladly accepted the cup. He drank. It was cold and clean and made him forget, for a moment, his troubles.

He wiped the milk mustache off his face. "Thanks."

Ethan didn't want to leave. It was a relief to be around someone who wasn't mad at him.

"Do you have time for a question?"

Dr. Irving said, "Of course."

"There's one thing I don't get about the I.C.E. suits. . . ."

This was the understatement of the century.

There were a gazillion things Ethan didn't understand. How could insects grow so big? How did the pilot-bug mental connection work? How did manufactured things like lasers and missiles and mechanical jet engines fit alongside organic things like muscles and insect organs?

One thing, though, *really* bothered him.

"When I'm in a suit . . ." Ethan faltered. He'd reminded himself he might *never* be in an I.C.E. suit again. He swallowed and went on. "I can punch through steel. I can take missiles and bombs exploding at point-blank range. How is that possible?"

Dr. Irving nodded in appreciation. "Clever to ask *that* question. That Ch'zar technology is the key to the entire I.C.E. system."

He closed the program he'd been working on. A password-protection shield splashed across the monitor. Dr. Irving quickly typed on his keyboard.

Ethan wasn't *supposed* to be looking, but he was standing right there . . . and his eyes just happened to be on the keyboard.

Dr. Irving typed *StormFalcon.*

The password shield vanished.

Ethan blushed. He shouldn't have seen that. He knew it was wrong. He didn't say anything, though. He didn't want Dr. Irving to be mad at him like everyone else.

On-screen, hundreds of spheres appeared and jostled into an ordered pattern.

"We only partially understand this technology," Dr. Irving explained. "The Ch'zar can change the density of the insect's exoskeleton."

The spheres on the computer squeezed together supertight.

"It takes enormous energies," Dr. Irving said, "but under life-threatening stress, or if a pilot is strong enough to mentally coax his bug to induce this transformation, a layer of insect armor only molecules thick can become a thousand times harder than diamond. It is tougher than yards of solid titanium. A teaspoon of such material would be so heavy, it would take our most powerful hydraulics to budge it an inch."

Ethan stared, fascinated.

No wonder he could rip through steel and stone as if it were wet tissue paper when he was inside an I.C.E. suit.

"You seem interested in the science," Dr. Irving said.

Ethan brightened. "I won blue ribbons at my school science fair—one for a robotic arm and one for the biology of the nerve. This stuff is light-years ahead of that. Yeah, you bet I'm interested!"

Ethan imagined himself designing new suits, insects that flew or burrowed or swam underwater. Could he make one that rocketed into outer space?

"I could use a bright assistant." Dr. Irving tapped his lower lip. "Perhaps in a few years, though." A serious look darkened his wrinkled face.

Ethan sighed and understood.

"In a few years" meant after Ethan had reached puberty . . . when he wouldn't be flying outside anymore.

If he was going to ever fly again after the incident with Paul.

There was a very real chance Ethan would never breathe fresh air again or feel the sun on his face.

As if he could read Ethan's thoughts, Dr. Irving said, "I could speak to Colonel Winter on your behalf."

He reached for the communication handset on his desk. Before he touched it, it buzzed.

The call code "099" glowed on the handset's display. It came from the base's Command and Control Center.

Dr. Irving frowned at it. He waved Ethan back and took the call.

"This is Dr. Irving. Yes, it is that dire."

He tapped on his keyboard.

The window showing the superdense molecules winked off. A new window opened. Dr. Irving glanced over his shoulder at Ethan and made another "back up, please" motion.

Ethan stepped away a respectful distance, but not before he glimpsed a map with red dots. It was the map that had been in Colonel Winter's office. The same one Dr. Irving and the other adult officers had stood around muttering things about "dire consequences" and "fallback contingencies."

Ethan was no military strategist, but even he knew this couldn't be good.

"There are no errors," Dr. Irving said into the handset. "Yes, I'll be right up."

Dr. Irving shut down his computer and stood. "I'm sorry, my boy. I've been summoned. We'll talk about biology and you helping me another day."

"Yes, sir."

Ethan wanted to remind Dr. Irving that he promised to talk to the colonel on his behalf, but for once the doctor looked every bit his age, his skin ashen, the sparkle in his eyes now a glassy sheen.

He smiled at Ethan, but it was a weak attempt to cover up his worry.

Something was seriously wrong here.

Dr. Irving left the laboratory as Madison walked in.

She almost bumped into him. They exchanged a few hushed words, he hugged her, and then he hurried on his way.

Seeing them side by side, Ethan noticed the same wicked intelligence reflect in their eyes. And that hug . . . they had to be related. Could he be her grandfather? Everyone else at the Seed Bank had grown up together and knew who was related to who. Not knowing simple, stupid things like that just made Ethan feel awkward . . . and like an outsider.

Madison glanced around the lab and her green eyes landed on Ethan. She scowled. "Blackwood. Just who I was looking for."

"What now?" Ethan said.

"The shower room is overflowing." Madison strolled over and snorted a laugh. "You need to get down there and clean it out."

Madison's nose was a smidge crooked and her hair was wild (spiked and sticking straight up today). There was something other than her weirdo looks, though, that made Ethan feel butterflies in his stomach when she was near.

He crossed his arms over his chest. "Me not flying and being on toilet duty is no joke, Madison."

"I know. Our roster was down a *bunch* of pilots with the flu already before you and Paul had to out-boy each other for Stupid of the Year award and get grounded."

She thought he was a pilot like Paul? Not a trainee? That was news to him.

Ethan didn't get her. How she could be mean one second and almost sweet the next. It reminded Ethan that the strangest alien species on Earth wasn't the Ch'zar—it was girls.

"Felix said he was going to try to talk to the colonel about it." Madison shook her head. "I don't know, though. She's really mad. You messed up pretty good."

"*I* messed up?"

She shrugged. "Well, Paul did . . . mostly. But you let him trick you into that race. What were you thinking?"

He hadn't been. Thinking, that is. He'd let his anger get the best of him.

But he didn't say *that* to Madison.

She sat on Dr. Irving's desk, leaned closer, and whispered, "Just get over it, will you? Something else is going on I wanted to talk to you about. Every officer on base shuts up whenever one of us gets near them."

"I know."

Ethan had seen that. And something was superwrong if it made Dr. Irving as worried as the rest of them.

He glanced over to the computer. "I think, though, I can find out what."

He sat and his fingers hovered over the keyboard.

Madison rolled her eyes. "Sure, what do you have to lose? Get thrown in the brig with Paul for *spying*. Not that it's going to do you any good. I've been trying for years to figure the password to my grandfather's comp—"

Ethan tapped in *StormFalcon*.

The computer screen flickered to life.

A map of the world covered with red dots came into focus.

Madison's and Ethan's mouths fell open at what they saw.

○ ○ ○ **7** ○ ○ ○

MORE NUMSKULL PILOTS

ETHAN AND MADISON STARED AT THE MAP
on the computer screen. North America had glowing
green outlines and the oceans burned with crisp blue
edges. Red dots were *everywhere*, though, like the conti-
nent had the measles. The dots clustered mostly near lakes
and rivers and valleys and a few places in the deserts.

There were none up in the Sierra Nevada, the Rock-
ies, or the Appalachian Mountains (where the Seed Bank
was hidden).

That made Ethan feel . . . safer.

He shut his open mouth.

Those dots were bad news. He didn't know why, but his brain churned just staring at them.

Madison leaned over his shoulder and whispered, "Is that what I think it is?"

"A map?"

"Duh!" She whacked him on the side of the head. "I can see that. I meant— Hey! How'd you get that password?"

Ethan ignored her question. There was no need to get into that right now.

"Dr. Irving said his numbers were right." Ethan continued to study the map. "I don't see numbers."

On the bottom of the screen was a menu.

He tapped a control to zoom in.

The image moved to the Florida coast, where there was an enormous cluster of red dots next to Lake Okeechobee in the Everglades. As the image grew, the tiny dots resolved in greater detail and looked like Egyptian hieroglyphics.

Only they weren't.

Ethan leaned forward. They were the outlines of insects.

Madison pushed him out of the seat and took over. "Let me drive, rookie." She typed in commands.

The gigantic holographic projector in the lab lit up.

The map on the computer materialized in midair, in full color, rivers and coastlines animated. Each red dot was a beach ball–sized sphere.

Ethan walked around the larger map and recognized several of the bug outlines. They were Ch'zar I.C.E. suits: the red-and-black assault wasps; the mosquitoes he'd fought in simulation; even Thunderbolt-class locusts.

He shuddered seeing that last one. A giant locust had almost torn off his arm at the Battle of Santa Blanca.

Ethan spotted one number on the bottom of the map. It was a date, two years ago.

He frowned. Dr. Irving had said *numbers*. Plural.

"Maybe if you zoom in more," he suggested to Madison.

She typed in commands.

A red insect symbol enlarged and split into a dozen. Next to each of those were numbers: 8, 5, 12 . . .

"Coordinates?"

"They're not latitude or longitude," Madison said. She stood up and strolled over to Ethan and the map.

The rotten feeling in Ethan's stomach finally, maybe, made sense. "What if they are just numbers," he whispered. "The number of Ch'zar units?"

Madison looked back and forth, and frowned as she

added them up. "That can't be. There are too many of them."

The date on the map popped to today's date.

The numbers next to the insect symbols jumped—13, 9, 25 . . .

The date rolled over one month, two months, three months into the future.

The numbers grew at an alarming rate—53 . . . 178 and 213 . . .

Suddenly Ethan felt nothing. He was numb. In shock.

By Christmas there could be *tens of thousands* of Ch'zar to fight.

Once before, he'd seen satellite images of the world and positions of these Ch'zar units . . . only then he'd guessed they were outnumbered ten or, at worst, a hundred to one.

Never *this* many.

Ethan imagined the sky covered with an endless carpet of black flying bugs, shaking the earth with their collective droning.

If they had any idea where the Resisters' Seed Bank base was, the last free-willed humans on the planet would be toast.

"How many do we have to fight them?" Ethan whispered. "I mean here. Resisters."

Madison was in a trance, her eyes full of the reflection of the map.

He gave her a shove. She snapped out of it, shot him an irritated glare, and one delicate hand involuntarily curled into a fist.

"We are *so* dead," she said. "We only have twenty-seven flight-ready pilots."

She looked angry and brave, but underneath, Ethan could see she was scared out of her mind.

Like him.

"Wait a second," Ethan said. "Just twenty-seven? I've seen hundreds of I.C.E. suits in the hangars."

"Don't be so thick, Blackwood. There are hundreds of *suits*. That's never been our problem. There're just so many of us born underground and free. And only about a third of the kids here have the mental strength to control the insect mind in an I.C.E. unit."

Ethan turned back to the map and lost himself in the sea of red bug symbols and numbers.

Even if they flew perfect missions against the enemy, had kill ratios of a hundred to one, they'd be vastly, enormously, *fatally* outnumbered.

"I'm beginning to rethink you," Madison muttered, looking at him through slitted eyes.

"What does *that* mean?"

"It means that even though you're a total pain, Blackwood, we could use a dozen more numskull, super-stubborn neighborhood kids like you to fight for us."

"I thought Dr. Irving said I was the only one from a neighborhood to ever get an I.C.E. suit to fly."

She didn't answer, staring at the map as if some new fact might pop up that would change the odds.

"What about Paul?" Ethan asked. "Colonel Winter said she should have 'left him where they found him.' What'd she mean by that?"

Madison faced Ethan, confusion crinkling her nose. "That's right. Paul isn't from the Seed Bank. No one said where he was from. It was this big secret. But we all stopped asking when we saw how he could fly."

They looked at each other—then at the computer terminal—and both raced to the keyboard.

Ethan got there first.

The way Paul acted, a total brat, Ethan bet he'd *never* been raised in a neighborhood. Wherever he came from . . . maybe there were more like him to help the Resistance.

He closed the map and transferred to a folder marked PERSONNEL.

The password shield splashed across the computer screen.

Ethan typed in Dr. Irving's code word, and it vanished.

There were hundreds of files with serial numbers.

Ethan opened them all.

Faces and birthdays and test scores spilled across the screen.

Madison, not content to watch, sat on the seat next to Ethan and scooched him to one side.

He felt her body heat next to him and inched away, uncomfortable.

Madison hit the command to sort the files. Her hand brushed over his, sending chills up Ethan's arm. It was strange because the feeling wasn't totally unwelcome. It was kind of . . . nice.

Too weird.

The files reorganized on-screen, and he snapped his attention back to their task.

His record popped to the top.

Place of birth: Santa Blanca.

Memories of a family, school, homework, soccer games—a normal life—flooded Ethan's thoughts.

He pushed them aside. He had to.

Besides, there had never been a "normal" anything in his life. It'd all been lies.

His Resister file had a picture of him taken after he

got out of boot camp. Any trace of baby fat that had once rounded his face had been pounded out of him by the physical training. He looked harder and meaner. He still had his dad's proud Cherokee jaw and his mom's smooth, golden Filipino skin, but he looked older . . . and there was something about the face that stared back at him that Ethan didn't recognize.

"Tab ahead," Madison told him. She reached for the key.

Ethan blocked her. "Wait, I want to read my file."

Madison looked like she was about to say something stupid, like this was "confidential," but then she pulled her hand back and looked away.

Ethan scanned his test flight scores (impressive), but then found:

status report on pilot trainee: Blackwood, Ethan Gregor
submitted to colonel winter, B., by corporal Irving, M.

Ethan, supercurious to know what Madison thought of him, skimmed ahead.

physical assessment: . . . Up to our standards. But barely.

skill assessment: . . . Great instincts in a dogfight.

comments (staff sergeant Hicks, P.) . . . Blackwood is a show-off . . . wants to prove he's better than anyone born in the Resistance. . . . He's going to get himself or his wingmates killed.

Ethan felt as if he were in a falling elevator—that dizzy, vertigo, out-of-body sensation.

Those last comments had to be Paul just hating his guts. He turned to Madison to ask what she really thought.

"It's true," Madison whispered before he could even ask. There was no anger in her voice. "You're a great pilot. Maybe the best I've ever seen. But *only* solo. If I put you on a squadron? On my team? I'd spend half my time watching out for whatever crazy stunt you'd pull next— instead of fighting the enemy."

Ethan barely heard her as he stared at the assessment on-screen.

recommendation: FAIL

Was he trying to prove he was as good as anyone else in the Resistance? Taking foolish risks to do it?

"Don't look like I just kicked you," she told him, somehow sounding hurt, too. "Read ahead. There's more."

She hit the NEXT PAGE button. On-screen appeared:

mitigating notes (corporal irving, m.):

Four weeks ago we recruited Blackwood into the Resistance.

He has had to accept: (1) Aliens kept his family and friends prisoners in the perfect neighborhood of Santa Blanca. (2) When kids reach puberty, their brain chemistry changes and they get absorbed into the aliens' mentally controlled Collective. (3) His parents were part of that uncaring Ch'zar Collective.

Boot camp was hard on Blackwood, too, especially the hand-to-hand combat classes (one tooth knocked out and replaced). Living in perfect, "safe" Santa Blanca just hasn't prepared him for this.

suggest he be reassessed after two weeks. Blackwood deserves a break.

Madison's extra comments didn't make Ethan feel any better about the overall recommendation, though. FAIL.

Was she right about that?

In soccer, Ethan *had* to be the star because he was the youngest and came from the smallest family in Santa Blanca. He'd struggled to get good grades because he wanted to be an astronaut and because he thought he didn't measure up to the other neighborhood kids.

Maybe he was just trying to do his best again here. And maybe other people were just seeing that as showing off.

Maybe.

"Whatever," he told her. His tone was icy.

Madison sighed and looked like she wanted to say more.

He turned away and tabbed ahead. "Let's just find Paul's record."

The next record had SEED BANK filled in for place of birth.

"Oh, for crying out loud," Madison said, and punched the FILE DOWN button a half-dozen times.

Paul Hicks's record sprang into view on-screen.

The place of birth was blank.

Ethan's heart practically stopped beating as he read what had been written *under* it.

"We have to talk to the colonel," he whispered. "This is *exactly* what we're looking for."

Under the empty place of birth entry was:

LAST KNOWN RESIDENCE:

STERLING REFORM SCHOOL

∘ ∘ ∘ 8 ∘ ∘ ∘

CLASS-A RESTRICTED

ETHAN HIT THE ELEVATOR CALL BUTTON for the thirteenth time in the last half hour.

Madison leaned against the corridor wall, her arms tightly crossed over her chest, and shifted from foot to foot. "This is moronic."

"We can't just stroll into C and C and talk to Colonel Winter," he told her. "In case you hadn't noticed, I'm not on her 'favorite person' list lately."

"So we're supposed to wait here and call *every* elevator coming down from the Command Center hoping she'll be on one? We'll be—"

The elevator bell pinged. The doors opened.

Colonel Winter stood inside. Alone.

"Well?" She frowned at them. "Are you two getting on or not?"

She looked distracted. Ethan didn't think she even recognized him.

"Yes, ma'am!" Ethan and Madison said together.

They stepped into the elevator, and the doors closed.

The *last* thing Ethan wanted to do was to talk to the colonel, but he had to. All their lives might depend on his plan.

He opened his mouth to speak, but Colonel Winter took a good look at him and finally realized who he was.

"Don't you have duties, Mr. Blackwood?"

"Yes, ma'am. Clogs in the semisolid waste facility. I was just on my way."

Technically this had been true—before he had made his discovery in Dr. Irving's lab.

"I was thinking, though, ma'am . . ."

Colonel Winter raised one eyebrow at him as if to say "thinking" might be a new activity for Ethan.

How did Felix stand that look? How hard was it for his friend to have the commander of a military base as a mother?

Ethan pressed on. "I was thinking we could really use some new pilots."

"What makes you think that, Mr. Blackwood?"

He had to be supercareful. Ethan couldn't say that he had seen Dr. Irving's dire Ch'zar population studies by hacking into a top-secret computer.

"Replacement pilots," Madison said, quickly covering for Ethan. "Because so many kids are out with the flu."

"I see . . . ," the colonel said.

"Dr. Irving told me that no other neighborhood kids had ever piloted an I.C.E. suit," Ethan said.

The colonel exhaled. She glanced at the numbers over the elevator's door, as if she was hoping this ride would soon end so she could get away from "troublemaker" Ethan Blackwood.

"There is another place where the kids"—Ethan cleared his throat—"might have the independent streak to make a good connection with the insect fighting suits."

The colonel's eyes locked on to Ethan.

"Sterling Reform School," he told her.

She took a step closer to Ethan. "And what do *you* know about *that* place?"

Ethan took an involuntary step back. He couldn't help but take a long look at the ivory-handled pistol strapped to her hip.

He took a deep breath and reminded the colonel how exactly he knew about Sterling Reform School.

Ethan had been shipped off to the place. After he discovered the truth about the Ch'zar (that his neighborhood wasn't the safe, happy place he'd thought), the mind-controlled adults of Santa Blanca captured him and put him on a bus for Sterling.

Before that, he'd heard rumors about the school growing up. He explained to the colonel that Sterling was where they sent the rule breakers and troublemakers. Some said it was where they sent kids who were mentally unstable and couldn't be treated.

On the bus ride, he'd seen a welcome video about Sterling. If the video could be believed, the kids there fought mock battles with padded sticks, exploded things in chemistry lab, and were actually *encouraged* to be out of control.

If it hadn't been for a last-minute rescue by Felix and Madison, that's where Ethan would be right now.

"It seems to me," Ethan said, "those are exactly the type of kids who could pilot I.C.E. suits. Why not rescue and recruit them?"

He very carefully left out that he knew that the Resister's star pilot, Paul Hicks (also apparently their star troublemaker), had come from Sterling.

The colonel punched the elevator's STOP button.

She stepped even closer to Ethan and told him, "Mr. Blackwood, I want to make myself perfectly, one hundred percent understandable on this. So if there's something you're not absolutely clear on, please ask."

Ethan gulped. Her fake nice tone made his spine crawl. "Yes, ma'am."

"Good," she said. "I'm giving you a direct order. You are not to mention the Sterling School to anyone else." She cast a glance at Madison. "That goes for you, too, Corporal Irving."

Colonel Winter hit the GO button. The elevator lurched ahead.

"In fact, Mr. Blackwood," she said, "I don't want you *thinking* about Sterling. Consider it a Class-A restricted site for all Resisters—especially Resister pilots, and especially Resister pilot trainees."

"I understand," Ethan managed to whisper.

He understood the order, but not the *reason* behind it.

What was so terrible about Sterling?

The elevator stopped and the doors opened. Cold air washed into the space. Outside was the landing hangar, busy with technicians working on I.C.E. suits and pilots clambering into and out of the cockpits.

Ethan wished he were out there.

The colonel stepped out and gestured to Madison. "I believe you have duties here, Corporal?"

"Yes, ma'am!" Madison scurried out after her, her spiked hair bobbing wildly. Madison shot Ethan a half-pleading look that warned him, *DON'T DO ANYTHING STUPID!*

Or, it might have been, *DON'T DO ANYTHING, STUPID!*

The doors closed.

Ethan slumped against the wall, feeling like he was going to pass out or throw up . . . maybe both.

That hadn't gone as he'd hoped with Colonel Winter.

From her reaction, though, he knew there *was* something special about Sterling.

But what?

How could she just ignore it when in a few months this base could very well be overrun by Ch'zar?

There was only one person here who had answers.

Ethan reached for the elevator's buttons but hesitated. Was this the right thing? Or was it like Madison had written in her assessment—that Ethan Blackwood was reckless and out to prove he was the best, no matter who it hurt?

No.

His instincts screamed at him that this was the *right* thing to do, the only thing.

If no one else was going to take action and save the Seed Bank and the Resisters, Ethan *had* to.

Even if it meant helping a person who wanted to kill him.

THE BREAK-IN

ETHAN PUSHED A CART FULL OF PLUNGERS, spools of steel cable that snaked through pipes, clog-dissolving chemicals, and cleaners to make everything spick-and-span.

It was completely humiliating.

A week ago he'd been learning to fly and fight with the best pilots on earth. Now he was a waste management tech, second class.

He'd missed out on an important mission. Jack Figgin and his squadron took a group of trainees out, crushed a Ch'zar security patrol, and hacked into an electronic relay in the enemy's satellite dish on Mount Rushmore. That gave the Resistance a new set of "eyes" in the air from Seattle to Chicago.

And what had Ethan been doing while all the excitement had been going on? Important things like mopping, learning to read plumbing blueprints, cleaning porcelain, and pushing his utility cart from toilet to toilet.

He hadn't realized that while being a pilot trainee was a tough job, it got him out of a lot of work the other Seed Bank kids did day after day. There were a hundred technical apprentices, maintenance workers, and agricultural engineers. Everyone over the age of eight had a job.

Sure, there were fun things to do, too: the game rooms, basketball tournaments, virtual tours of places aboveground, a huge library, and, of course, school.

Ethan had been shunned, though.

It wasn't just his job (the most undesired, smelly post on base). Everyone knew he and Paul had gotten into deep trouble. People went out of their way to ignore him.

The one good thing about this situation was that the colonel's punishment gave him the perfect excuse to go almost anywhere unnoticed on base.

Including the brig.

Ethan wheeled the cart down a dank corridor to the prison cell block.

At the end of the hall was a Plexiglas enclosure. Inside, a bored guard watched a bank of computer monitors. He was older than Ethan, maybe eighteen, and had sergeant stripes on his blue coverall uniform.

He looked up and snickered. "Hey, rookie," the guard called out. "You come here to fly one of our toilets?"

"Yeah, that's funny, Sergeant," Ethan told him. "It's going to be *hilarious* when your toilets overflow. You'll be ankle-deep in the stuff."

That shut him up.

The guard opened an impressively thick steel door and came to inspect Ethan and his cart. Everything was exactly as it looked: one pilot trainee on probation toilet duty and one cart full of plumbing tools and supplies.

All part of Ethan's plan.

"Exactly what's the problem?" the guard asked. He didn't look convinced. "I didn't see a report."

"I didn't think you would," Ethan said. His heart pounded. He wasn't good at lying. It'd been strictly against the rules back in his Santa Blanca life, but he figured a good way to lie was to start with the truth.

"There's a problem in the semisolid waste processing plant," he said, trying to sound like he didn't care. "A blockage somewhere between here and there."

The guard scratched his head. "So?"

"I was going to clear it from this end before the pressure backed everything out."

This wasn't a lie—just an unlikely scenario. The guard didn't know that, though.

"But"—Ethan turned the cart around—"if you want me to ask the engineers to file a report first."

"Wait." The guard grabbed the cart. "Just fix it, rookie. Now."

Ethan took out a map of the plumbing lines. "Let me figure out where I need to go."

The guard held open the steel security door as Ethan wheeled his cart into the cell block. The walls were welded steel plates. It was cold and smelled of rust. Fluorescent lights flickered overhead.

Ethan didn't like the feel of this place, but he guessed that was the point.

They passed one cell door, and another, and another as he pretended to consult his blueprint of the plumbing lines. Ethan glanced through the tiny window on the next door and halted.

Paul Hicks was inside, sitting on a cot, reading a book.

What *was* Ethan doing? Risking everything on Paul Hicks? The one person here who genuinely hated him?

Yes. He had to, because Paul was the only person who'd ever been to the Sterling Reform School and become a Resister.

"This is the spot," Ethan whispered, hoping he didn't sound as terrified as he felt.

The guard hesitated, looked at Paul, and then to Ethan. He shrugged, took out a set of keys, and unlocked the cell door.

Ethan exhaled. So far so good.

Now the hard part. He tugged on the cap he wore, pulling it low over his face.

"Hicks," the guard growled. "This guy's going to fix the toilet."

"It works fine," Paul muttered without looking up from his book, *All Quiet on the Western Front.*

"Well, it's not *going* to work if he doesn't do his job. Don't get in his way."

"Whatever," Paul said.

Ethan pushed the cart into the cell.

"I'll be back at my station," the guard told Ethan. He motioned at the ceiling's corner where a camera pointed into the cell. "I'll be watching," he said, loudly enough so Paul could hear. "Don't let the prisoner give you any trouble. Yell if he starts anything."

Ethan nodded.

The guard closed and locked the door behind him.

Ethan's insides wobbled. He was more nervous than if he'd been about to fly into a swarm of Ch'zar.

He was trapped in a prison cell with his mortal enemy. Would Paul beat him up? He might feel like he had nothing to lose. More important, would Paul give Ethan enough time to explain himself? And then . . . would he believe him?

Leaning on his cart so his knees didn't buckle, Ethan wheeled it to the toilet.

Paul ignored him and kept reading.

In case the guard was watching, Ethan went through the motions of plunging and then got out the metal snake and shoved it down the pipe.

"I came to tell you a few things," Ethan whispered to Paul. "Listen. But don't look up."

Paul looked up.

His eyes widened, he dropped his book, and he set a foot on the floor like he was about to jump at Ethan. His mouth curled into a snarl.

But then he froze and glanced back at the camera.

Ethan guessed he was doing a mental calculation: how many times would he be able to pound Ethan's head into the toilet before the guard came and pulled him off?

"I need your help," Ethan hissed at him. "Not for me,

but for the base—for everyone. I don't like you, Hicks. I tried to be nice to you and got punched in the nose for my trouble. But you know things that I need to know."

Still angry, Paul pursed his lips, but the murderous glint in his eyes cooled.

"Well, Blackwood," he whispered, "you've got my attention. You must have something awfully important to say to sneak in here." He picked up his book, leaned back, and pretended to read. "You've got fifteen seconds before I finish the job I started last week in the hangar."

Ethan wanted to ask Paul what his problem was. They were both already up to their ears in hot water, and he was willing to get in deeper? Just to get even with Ethan for saving his life?

What a jerk.

Ethan pushed his anger aside. There were more important things to tell Paul.

He started with Dr. Irving's Ch'zar population projections.

"*You* hacked into Dr. Irving's computer?" Paul asked, leaning forward, grinning so the scars on his face stretched.

Ethan carefully didn't answer that and got to the part where the Resisters were outnumbered about a thousand to one . . . and would soon be outnumbered a hundred thousand to one if they didn't do something.

The nothing-scares-me-I'm-a-fighter-pilot expression on Paul's face faded.

"You're kidding."

"Madison was there. She can tell you."

Paul looked around. "Madison's not stupid enough to come down here to tell me anything."

Ethan continued his story—how he'd been the only neighborhood kid to ever fly I.C.E. armor, how he figured it had to be partly the pilots' stubbornness and independence that let them dominate the insect brains of the fighting suits.

"You *just* figured that out?" Paul muttered. "You're a genius, Blackwood."

Ethan pressed on. "I thought, 'Where else could we find more pilots to even the odds?' That's when I dug into *your* background."

Paul drew in a deep breath and shook his head as if he knew what Ethan was about to say.

"You're from Sterling Reform School," Ethan said. "That place must be full of kids—dangerous kids—with independent minds who could fight on our side. Even a few could make a big difference if they were half as good a pilot as you."

It took a lot for Ethan to admit Paul was a good pilot. But he was.

The compliment, though, didn't even register with Paul. The color drained from his face.

"No way," he whispered. "I barely got away from that place the first time."

Paul didn't look like a great fighter pilot anymore. He looked like a scared little kid.

Ethan explained how he'd tried to tell Colonel Winter, and how she'd shot down his plans.

He took a step closer to Paul. "That's exactly why I need you. I think you know where Sterling is. You know what goes on there—how well it's guarded. You got out once. We wouldn't go in unprepared. We'll have I.C.E. backup. Satellite uplink support. Weapons. And we know how to fight the Ch'zar."

Paul stared at Ethan as if he'd suggested they eat a handful of live, squirming worms.

"We need those kids," Ethan urged. "If we don't do anything, we'll get creamed by the Ch'zar in a few months."

Paul considered, looked Ethan straight in the eye, and laughed.

"You have real guts, coming down here. Your crazy plan, bucking the colonel's orders . . . I've got to give it to you, Blackwood." He picked up his book and started reading again. "But Madison was right: you're *all* guts and *no* brains."

Madison had said that? It irked Ethan she'd talked about him behind his back.

"Are you in?" Ethan asked. "Or are you too scared to even try?"

"Sure, I'm in," Paul said, like this was one big joke to him. "Assuming we could break out a bunch of those Sterling punks, assuming they turned out to be good enough to not *die* the first time they fly against the Ch'zar, and assuming we weren't court-martialed and shot by Colonel Winter, you're overlooking two small details."

"Which are?"

"One: we don't have I.C.E. suits. And two"—Paul gestured helplessly around him—"in case you hadn't noticed, I'm in jail."

Ethan smiled.

"That's why I'm here. I'm going to break you out."

∘ ∘ ∘ 10 ∘ ∘ ∘

THE BREAKOUT

ETHAN RUMMAGED THROUGH HIS CART AND
pulled out a large syringe marked

DRAIN CLEANER

WARNING: <u>EXTREMELY</u> CAUSTIC!

A plumbing engineer had showed Ethan how it mixed
two chemicals as it was injected. It made a superdissolving
cocktail that chewed through any clog. He'd been warned
not to use it on the base's softer steel pipes because it
would completely dissolve them.

Ethan marched to the cell door, turned his back to the camera (to block its view), and squirted a blob of the viscous chemicals into the keyhole.

Paul gaped at him, confused, intrigued, and then like he thought Ethan was *nuts*.

"I'll be back in a few minutes," Ethan whispered. "Figure out a way to hide from the camera, stuff a few pillows under the blankets so it looks like you're sleeping, and be ready to go!"

Paul nodded, finally understanding that Ethan was *really* going to break him out.

Or at least try.

Ethan felt butterflies again in his stomach, this time a flock of them about to take wing.

He waved up to the camera and called out, "I'm done."

The guard came and opened the cell door.

He didn't notice the wisp of smoke that drifted from the keyhole.

"I'll need to check a few more toilets." Ethan pointed down the hallway at two cells.

"Sure," the guard said. "Those are empty and unlocked. Let me know when you're done and I'll escort you out."

Ethan pushed his cart down the corridor and went through the motions of plunging and cleaning those two other toilets to give the drain cleaner time to eat through the lock on Paul's door.

Even though adrenaline pounded through his body and made him want to grab Paul and make a dash for it, he forced himself to be slow and careful.

As he walked back down the corridor, he spotted another camera.

He spritzed the lens with glass cleaner. That would fog the guard's view for a minute before it evaporated.

Time enough for him to break a *hundred* regulations . . .

Ethan stopped at Paul's cell door and tapped it once.

With a slight metal grinding, it opened.

Paul glanced around. He waited for an explanation as to how they were going to march past the guard.

Ethan opened the large trash can in his cart and gestured for Paul to get inside.

Paul flashed him a look. Admiration? The beginning of a great friendship?

Not a chance.

Ethan recognized *that* particular look. It said, *If you blow this, Blackwood, I'm going to pound your face flat—no matter how long the colonel throws me in the brig.*

He tossed soggy papers over Paul's head.

"Gross," Paul whispered.

Ethan tried not to smile as he locked the trash can's lid over Paul.

With a grunt, he pushed the now-much-heavier cart toward the guard station. His pulse thundered in his ears.

The guard ignored him as he approached the door.

They were almost out. He couldn't believe he was going to get away with this.

"Hang on!" the guard shouted.

Ethan froze.

Had he seen what he'd done on another camera? Or would he look though his cart? Even a casual search would blow everything.

The guard walked past Ethan, unlocked the steel security door, and held it open for him.

Ethan blinked, not quite understanding.

The guard gestured him through, and somehow Ethan pushed the cart forward.

"Have a great day, rookie," the guard called after him.

Ethan got to the elevator and waited for what seemed like forever for the car to arrive. The doors finally opened, and he wheeled the cart inside. He almost fell over when the doors closed.

He unlocked the trash can, and Paul clambered out, shaking off wet strips of toilet paper that clung to his back and sandy hair.

"So what now, genius?" he demanded. "We've got maybe an hour before the guard serves me lunch—*if* they're stupid enough to fall for that pillow-under-the-blanket trick."

"Don't worry," Ethan said (although nothing but worry churned inside him). "I've got everything figured out. I've done this before."

"You've *what*?"

Ethan wasn't going to explain that he'd stolen an I.C.E. suit before to fly back to Santa Blanca and save his sister, Emma. It hurt too much to think about it. He'd gotten away with the theft, successfully battled the Ch'zar (demolishing his old elementary school in the process), but the aliens had *still* taken Emma.

The elevator stopped and the doors opened.

Beyond was a hangar filled with I.C.E. suits, some torn apart and under repair—limbs detached, abdomens splayed out.

It reminded Ethan of his biology class. On dissection day.

"The techs are on break," Ethan whispered. "We have ten minutes before they're back from coffee."

Ethan had this perfectly timed, but so many things could go wrong. The technicians could come back early.

A random guard might wander through the repair hangar. Or there could be some hidden security camera.

He unzipped his coveralls. Underneath he wore his gold-and-black flight suit.

"Come on," he whispered to Paul. "Don't be such a chicken."

Ethan slunk out of the elevator.

Paul followed him. He grabbed a green-and-black flight suit from a locker and changed. Ethan noticed more scars on Paul's back and legs. He'd been through a lot of tough scrapes.

"Your I.C.E. is there." Ethan gestured to the wicked-looking praying mantis silhouette. "Mine's—"

"Hold on a second," a voice boomed from the shadows.

Felix and Madison stepped out. Both had their arms crossed over their chests. Madison looked like a tiny toy standing next to Felix's weight-lifter body.

"I told you he'd be stupid enough to try something like this," Madison muttered.

"I can't believe I took that bet with you," Felix whispered to her. He strode to Ethan and Paul, his hands up in a halt gesture. "This has got to end here, you two."

"Didn't Madison tell you about Dr. Irving's Ch'zar population study?" Ethan said.

Felix frowned. "That could be theoretical for all we know."

"Come on," Paul said. "When has Old Fossil Irving ever done anything theoretical that didn't turn out to be right?"

Madison marched forward, fingers rolling into fists, ready to slug Paul for calling her grandfather an old fossil.

Ethan stepped in front of Paul to shield him from her. "If it's all theoretical," he said, "why is every officer whispering about the 'dire situation' and 'fallback contingencies'? There's no fallback from the Seed Bank. You guys know what'll happen to any adult who leaves." Ethan turned to Felix. "You know what'll happen to your mom."

Felix recoiled.

That was a cheap shot to take.

Ethan took it, though, because it was true.

Colonel Winter, Dr. Irving—every adult Resister— were stuck here. If the Ch'zar discovered the secret base, the adults would either die fighting or get absorbed into the collective hive mind.

Felix's frown deepened into a scowl. It looked wrong on the boy's normally easygoing features. "So what are we going to do about it?" he asked Ethan.

"*We?*" Madison blurted. "Is Blackwood's insanity *catching?*"

She shoved Felix aside and blocked Ethan and Paul from their I.C.E. armor. "You got away with stealing a suit before because of a technicality. You were a civilian. You're part of the Resistance now. Colonel Winter wouldn't even bother with a court-martial. She might just order you guys blasted out of the air!"

"I'd like to see someone try," Paul told her, and stuck out his chin.

Ethan elbowed him. He wasn't helping.

"What do you want us to do?" Ethan asked Madison. "The adults are just trying to protect everyone here—I get that. But what if the *only* chance we have is to do something stupid and risky?"

Madison snorted. "You're the expert on that," she said, unconvinced.

"So what, then?" Ethan demanded. "We wait here? Let the Ch'zar breed and multiply and eventually zero in on the Seed Bank? We'll fly carefully planned, cautious missions, and probably get picked off one by one. And it'll end—not just for the Resistance, but for *every* human everywhere."

Across the hangar, a few medical monitors hooked up to I.C.E. suits beeped, but otherwise it was silent.

Madison nodded. "Yeah, okay, so . . . what's the plan?"

"Sterling Reform School," Ethan said.

Felix's eyes widened. "That's a Class-A restricted zone, Ethan."

"Good," Ethan replied, "then you know the place. We break out as many kids as we can. There have to be dozens there with the right mind-set to pilot our I.C.E. suits."

"Maybe hundreds," Paul said. He glanced away, though, suddenly evasive.

Was there more to Sterling kids than just an independent streak?

"Imagine if we had three or four or even five extra squadrons to fight the Ch'zar," Ethan said. "They could run interference while we bomb a few of the breeding nests. At the very least, we buy the Resisters time to think."

Madison and Felix looked at one another. A silent conversation flashed between them.

Maybe it was years of flying and fighting together, but Ethan could almost hear them arguing the pros and cons of his reasoning.

And then they both agreed.

"For the next few minutes," Felix said, straightening his uniform, "I'm officially still on duty. We can use that." He pulled out a data pad and tapped it. "There. I transferred Madison, myself, and Ethan onto the 'flu quarantine list.' That might give us an hour before anyone discovers we've gone AWOL."

AWOL stood for "absent without leave" in military jargon. It was a court-martialable offense according to the regulations.

As if Ethan hadn't already committed a dozen court-martialable crimes today.

It was his friends, though, that he worried about.

Madison piped in, "Just in case, we took the precaution of getting all our I.C.E. suits prepped, and we got a luna moth assault carrier." She nodded behind Ethan.

He turned.

Ethan hadn't seen the moth until now because the dusky gray-and-green camouflaging blended so well with the shadows. Only the faint silver-blue bioluminescent "eye spots" on the wings and safety lights on the abdomen gave the huge assault carrier away. The luna moth was the size of school bus and could carry a hundred people in utter silence. He'd heard it had been engineered for a mass rescue of neighborhood kids by the previous base commander, but for some reason that mission had never happened.

It wasn't fast, but it was superstealthy. The moth could be tethered mentally to one of their I.C.E. suits so it'd follow them. Ethan was happy to have it. It would give them the option of rescuing a lot of Sterling kids.

"Wait," Ethan said, his forehead furrowing with shock. "You had the suits ready?"

"Well," Madison said, looking to the deck, embarrassed, "just in case your plan wasn't *completely* nuts, we knew you'd need us."

Ethan felt a surge of gratitude. Madison and Felix had thought he might be right. They trusted him enough to follow him . . . even if he was breaking regulations, even if it meant getting court-martialed, or maybe even shot.

He wouldn't let them down.

He couldn't. Ethan was gambling with all their lives.

○ ○ ○ 11 ○ ○ ○

NO GOING BACK

BREAKING PAUL OUT OF JAIL, JAMMING their suits' transponder signals so they'd be harder to track, and sneaking off base—that was easy.

Ethan had even been ready for some secret recall code programmed into their suits that the officers could trigger and fly them back to base.

What he hadn't been prepared for, though, was to fly right into a swarm of Ch'zar Ranger-class reconnaissance honeybees the split second after their view screens turned on after the mandatory Security Protocol 003 blackout.

The all-steel insects had blackened barbs riveted to their limbs and particle-beam focusing antennae.

A swarm of ten units scattered before them.

They must've been just as surprised as Ethan that four Resister pilots had flown straight into their V formation.

Green energy beams blasted Ethan's wasp.

Overheat warnings blared on half his systems.

Before he was literally broiled inside his suit, Ethan dove to escape the barrage. He arced up, rolled, and banked to reengage the enemy.

His cockpit cameras tried to track every target, but the screens were a jumble of buzzing wings, blurred bodies, and the blue flash of a high-energy weapon. Ethan couldn't even tell who was shooting at whom. It was too much to follow.

He wanted to jump right back into battle (or maybe it was his connection to his wasp's "killer" brain), but Ethan had to slow down, take it all in, and figure out the right strategy.

He wasn't about to die three minutes into his mission.

There were bees everywhere.

They had the advantage of numbers. All they had to do was refocus their formation, isolate one of Ethan's squadron, and take them out one by one.

"Madison," Ethan said over the radio. "Fly *through* the

center as they regroup. Shoot anything that moves. Paul, Felix, fall back and let her string them out."

"Who put you in charge?" Paul shouted back.

"Just do it," Madison said.

She kicked on her afterburners and her emerald-green dragonfly left a bloom of white vapor as it went supersonic.

Madison plowed through the regrouping bees.

Her lasers flashed. Three of the enemy insects dropped, metal bodies smoldering and wings singed.

She left the bees struggling to stay airborne in her turbulence.

They turned and pursued . . . or tried to.

Madison's dragonfly was the fastest thing in the air.

"Go now!" Ethan shouted to Paul and Felix. "Hit them with everything you've got while they're separated."

Ethan had almost forgotten about the luna moth assault carrier! He looked for it on his radar. He didn't find it, but he *did* see the three bees chasing after *something*.

The assault carrier's shadowy stealth surfaces prevented radar lock-ons, but its autopilot was limited. It was only programmed to fly straight away from danger.

The bees must have a visual on it.

Meanwhile, Felix's rhinoceros beetle fired its heavy

particle beam—a lightning-bright white-blue bolt of energy that blasted bees into smoldering bits of shrapnel. Paul's praying mantis grabbed one straggler bee and then another, and smashed them together, and in a show of unnecessary violence, the mantis bit off one bee's head.

Ethan rocketed after the vulnerable luna moth.

He closed and fired his laser at the nearest bee. The beam sliced through where the wing joined the carapace. It tumbled out of control and plummeted to the ground.

The other two bees slowed, turned, and fired at him.

A particle beam splashed over his chest.

The cockpit got hot. It was hard to breathe. Air vents screamed and tried to cool the interior. A hydraulic pressure gauge exploded and showered the cockpit with metal and glass bits, cutting Ethan's cheek.

He couldn't stop. Ethan couldn't let them get to the moth. That was the only way they were going to rescue the Sterling kids.

He tapped his afterburners and crashed into one of the bees.

His wasp wrestled with the bee. Ton for ton, it was a match for him—and just as ferocious.

The second bee latched on to him. It grabbed one of his wings.

That was bad.

If they tore a wing off, there was nothing he could do to stay in the air.

The wasp slashed out with its barbed forelegs. Its laser shot uselessly into the air. Nothing worked! The bees were just out of reach.

Ethan rolled and wobbled but couldn't shake them.

This wasn't like any simulation he'd run in the last few weeks. Ethan felt panic rise through his chest. He wanted to scream.

A ghostly translucent green covered one camera.

It was Paul.

His praying mantis repositioned, grabbed one of the bees with its hooked forelimbs, and tore the bee in half.

The last bee flew off.

Felix instantly blasted it into smoldering blobs of molten metal. He'd lined up the perfect shot with his heavy particle beam.

The praying mantis clung to the back of Ethan's wasp.

"Now we're even, Blackwood," Paul said over the radio, and shoved the wasp away.

The wasp's instinct to engage the praying mantis and fight it to the death flooded Ethan's mind.

He took a deep breath and forced that urge into the dark recesses of the insect's mind.

At least, he hoped it was *just* the wasp's mind and not his.

Ethan wiped the blood off his face with a shaking hand. He took a second to regain his bearings and fly level.

There was a weird shudder in the wasp's right wing. He didn't like that.

Madison whispered over the radio, "Long-range radar picking up more enemy patrols. I've never seen so many, so close."

"Go terrain-level flight," Felix said in his no-nonsense command voice. "Exit the region. Something probably saw the explosions. Maintain radio silence until further notice."

The five I.C.E. units dove in formation and accelerated over the treetops.

The shudder in Ethan's wing settled into a minor but persistent rattle.

Of course, at five hundred miles an hour, a little rattle could end up ripping his hull into confetti.

He kept quiet.

Stopping for repairs would put the entire team, and the mission, at risk.

There was no stopping now. There was no going back.

○ ○ ○ 12 ○ ○ ○

CODE RED

THEY FLEW DOWN FROM THE APPALACHIAN
Mountains, over rolling green fields in Tennessee, and
then thundered across Texas grasslands and deserts.

Ruins studded the horizon to the south: rusting skyscrapers and cracked crystal spires.

What mysteries lay buried in the graveyard of human
civilization? Ethan wanted to explore what the world had
been like before the Ch'zar, but Knucklebone Canyon
had almost crumbled on top of him and Paul, and it'd
been infested with those black widows. Just thinking
about those spiders made Ethan's skin crawl.

He flew on.

Maybe after this mission, after they'd beaten back the Ch'zar, he could explore . . . *if* there was anything left there to find.

A map of the next region flashed on-screen. Green circles dotted the Arizona and Nevada desert. It wasn't a friendly green either. It was the vile fluorescent green of skull-and-crossbones poison warning labels.

Ethan's radio link blinked amber. It was receiving an encrypted short-range signal. He tapped it to decode and accept.

"We're approaching radiation zones," Felix said over the radio. "The Ch'zar cleaned up a bunch of them. Some, though, are too hot for even them to touch."

Ethan was about to ask why the Ch'zar had bombed the world. Hadn't they used mind control fifty years ago to take over?

Then he got it: *they* hadn't bombed anyone.

Humans had done it to each other.

Felix and Madison had once told Ethan about World War IV, when people had almost annihilated each other, right before the Ch'zar came.

What would have happened if the aliens hadn't shown up? Would the entire world be a radioactive cinder?

Paul marked a spot on their map with an X.

"Fiesta City," he said over the radio. "That's our destination."

Ethan zoomed in on the satellite image.

There were lakes and parks and a city grid. It was an oasis in the vast desert.

He turned on his external cameras and magnified.

Was that a Ferris wheel lit against the setting sun? There were strings of flashing carnival lights. Neon was everywhere. He wasn't sure what all the crazy lights were about. He had a feeling this place wouldn't be like his Santa Blanca neighborhood.

"I thought we were looking for Sterling Reform School," Ethan said to Paul.

"It's in the middle of the city," Paul replied. His usual anger was gone, and there was a hint of fear in his voice.

"Fireflies patrolling the region," Madison said, interrupting. "They run like clockwork. We'll only be able to approach within six miles before they'll detect us."

"There's a dry riverbed south of the city," Paul said. "There are eroded overhangs. One should be big enough to hide our suits."

"Madison, scout it out," Felix said. "We need to make repairs . . . and talk."

Madison's dragonfly zipped into the dry river channel and disappeared. A moment later she said, "Found one."

They followed her down and banked along the contours of the dry river. Ethan spotted a shadow-filled undercut that concealed a cave the size of a house.

He landed and clambered out of his cockpit. It was good to breathe fresh air again.

Ethan couldn't enjoy it, though, because he had to check that wing rattle. He ran a hand over his wasp's gold armor. Tiny insect hairs bristled at his touch.

Flashes of ripping into enemy bugs and shooting its stinger laser filled Ethan's mind. The wasp didn't want to be done fighting.

Ethan tried to calm the insect, wishing it was a little less hostile.

Maybe it had to be that way. It had been born and bred to fight. Those instincts kept them both alive in the air. But was that all there was for the creature? Ethan actually felt sorry for the insect.

He found the damage on the wasp's wing. There was just a nick in the chitin-ceramic alloy. If it wasn't fixed, though, it'd become a tear, and the wing could eventually rip off in flight.

Felix came over and gave Ethan a towel-sized yellow bandage. It had red stripes . . . and it rippled.

Ethan recoiled.

It was one of those flat caterpillar things. It was alive. It squirmed as he took it.

One had been slapped on him when his leg had been punctured. The thing cleaned and repaired the wound, but it was gross.

"These have cartilage protein binders to fix that nick," Felix told him. He laced his thick fingers together to demonstrate.

Ethan nodded and smoothed the bandage over the wing. The caterpillar stuck with a wet smacking noise and wiggled into place.

The wasp shifted, annoyed at the creature's presence.

"I know exactly how you feel," he said to his wasp.

Ethan glanced up and saw Madison inspecting her dragonfly. Her bodysuit rippled with the same camouflage greens of the insect. She lovingly ran her hands over its shell and patted it as if it were a pet. She had an entirely different relationship with her I.C.E. suit.

Madison . . . Ethan honestly didn't know what to think about her. She'd filed that failing flight assessment to Colonel Winter, but then she'd added those mitigating remarks. And then she'd had their suits fueled, charged, and loaded with field supplies. She *must* have believed in Ethan.

He owed her.

Madison looked up, flipped her hair out of her face (the gelled spikes had lost their stiffness on the flight out here), and glared at Ethan as if she could feel him thinking about her.

Ethan's face burned and he turned away.

Meanwhile, Felix directed the giant luna moth assault carrier, one hand on its thorax, so it sat between the other I.C.E. suits and the mouth of the overhang. The moth's stealth surfaces would deflect any signals from those firefly patrols.

Felix turned to them. "Okay, let's figure out our plan."

"You're not in charge of this mission, *Corporal*," Paul said. He cocked his head and seemed to be waiting for Felix to step aside.

"Sorry, Paul," Felix told him, "I *am* in charge. Technically you're not a staff sergeant. Escaped prisoners have no rank."

Paul shut up. He crossed his arms and fumed.

"Besides," Felix whispered, "there's something going on with you and this mission. I hear it in your voice. Am I wrong?"

Paul shuffled his feet. "It's just this place. It gives me . . . nightmares."

Felix waited for more explanation from Paul. None came.

Madison grabbed a backpack from her dragonfly's cockpit. "You two should stop arguing about who's going to lead," she said. "We should just get going!"

"We're not going anywhere without a plan," Felix said, his tone turning frosty. "And not without establishing a chain of command."

Madison rummaged in her pack and pulled out four baseball caps.

"Yeah," she said with a snort, "we need a chain of command for a mission that's illegal and probably the last thing we do before we all get court martialed."

She tossed Ethan a cap.

"What are these for?" he asked.

"Your head, stupid." Paul tugged one on.

"They're disguises," Felix told him. "The Ch'zar have seen us—especially you, Ethan. Every adult on the planet will recognize you because of their collective hive mind." He pointed to his iron-gray eyes. "They seem to know our eyes more than any other feature."

Ethan thought about *every* Ch'zar-controlled human adult on Earth knowing what he looked like and decided to *not* think about it.

Too creepy.

He turned the cap around. There was an embroidered red *R* on its crown.

"We stole them from a neighborhood baseball team called the Rebels." Madison smiled crookedly. "Rebels? Resisters? Get it? Just like us. I'd love to flaunt it in front of the Ch'zar."

Ethan smiled back, but he wasn't looking at the cap. He stared at the Resister pilot's wings on Madison's bodysuit.

He wished for the millionth time that he had a set of those. The insignia had crossed insect wings with a bundle of arrows underneath, all surrounded by a semicircle of gold stars. Only those who graduated from flight school got them, awarded in a special ceremony by Colonel Winter herself.

All things considered, it seemed awfully unlikely he'd get a set of those wings now (especially from Colonel Winter).

"Infiltration into Fiesta City won't be a problem," Paul told them. "We can walk right in."

"Hello? There are patrols," Madison said.

"Sterling kids walk out here all the time. The adults don't care." Paul gestured around them. "We're surrounded by radioactive desert. No one wanders too far."

Ethan saw similarities to this place and Santa Blanca. His old neighborhood wasn't surrounded by radioactive desert, but mountains. Both places were prisons.

A static squawk from Ethan's cockpit made everyone jump.

"Sorry," he said, his heart pounding from the unexpected noise. "I left the encrypted channel open."

Colonel Winter's voice filled the tiny cavern.

They all froze and listened.

"Broadcasting on cycling encrypted frequency Delta. This is a code red recall order to all units in the field. Repeat: a CODE RED recall order to all field units. This is not a drill. This is Santa Claus broadcasting on cycling encrypted frequency Delta. . . ."

Santa Claus was Colonel Winter's code name.

Code red meant there was an emergency—a big one. Every pilot, every ground unit, every Resister *everywhere* was supposed to get back to the Seed Bank as fast as they could.

The kids looked at each other, none sure what to do about the message.

"A code red means us," Felix whispered. "We've got to get back." He took a step toward his mother's voice.

"No way!" Paul maneuvered between him and the radio. "That's a trick."

"The colonel doesn't play tricks," Madison told him.

"She doesn't trick her *pilots*," Felix said, and frowned. "But maybe she doesn't think we're her pilots anymore. Maybe she thinks we're traitors . . . or we've changed." His gaze unfocused.

"That's ridiculous." Madison poked Felix in the ribs to get his attention. "If we changed, if the Ch'zar controlled us, we wouldn't be listening to any orders."

Ethan marched to his I.C.E. suit and turned off the radio. He sealed the cockpit.

"I hate to admit it," Ethan said, "but Paul's right. It could be a trick."

Paul seemed irritated that Ethan was agreeing with him.

"It doesn't matter," Ethan said. "It just means our mission is more important than ever. So the Resistance needs pilots. We're here to get them."

Felix smoothed a hand over his shorn hair. "Okay," he said, "we'll do the mission. We'll get these Sterling kids and get back as quick as possible."

"No argument with that," Paul said. He rummaged though his pack, found jeans and a T-shirt, and pulled them on over his flight suit. He shouldered the backpack and walked onto the dry riverbed. "You guys have no idea the trouble we're marching into."

Ethan wasn't sure what bothered him the most: seeing Paul walk off into the moonlit night after that cryptic warning—the urgency he'd heard in Colonel Winter's voice still echoing in his head—or the fact that they were walking into a Ch'zar prison stronghold with no backup.

He got the feeling they were marching into the absolute wrong place.

∘ ∘ ∘ 13 ∘ ∘ ∘

THE ABSOLUTE WRONG PLACE

ETHAN'S JEANS AND T-SHIRT FIT LOOSELY over his flight suit. It felt as if he wore a raincoat *under* his clothes. His boots crunched over gravel in the dry river-bed. In the moonlight the stones looked like bones.

Paul led the way, preferring to walk ahead.

Madison and Felix flanked Ethan.

No one spoke.

It was as if they were all afraid the Ch'zar might hear them.

Which was ridiculous because, of course, they were going to see and hear them coming. Those firefly patrols had to have spotted them. A hundred interceptor drones could be rocketing toward them right now.

How in the world was this going to work? Who took walks out in the wilderness in the middle of the night?

Then again, maybe it would work.

Over the bank of the dry riverbed, flashing lights and colors painted the night sky under Fiesta City.

If Ethan were in Santa Blanca, everyone would be settling down for dinner and then getting ready for bed. This place seemed to be just waking up.

Thinking of Santa Blanca made Ethan homesick.

Where was his sister Emma?

The Ch'zar had taken her away. She'd seen the battle in Santa Blanca, Resister I.C.E. suits fighting with Ch'zar giant insects. They probably put her in some work camp, if she hadn't hit puberty.

Puberty was when you had a growth spurt, started dating (which made Ethan uneasy just thinking about it), and pimples showed up on your face in force.

It was also when your brain changed, especially a part of the brain called the prefrontal cortex. When the prefrontal cortex changed, it became possible for the Ch'zar to mentally control humans. Emma could be part of the Ch'zar right now.

Thinking of *that* made Ethan feel sick.

It was a fate that awaited them all if they couldn't beat the Ch'zar.

The only exception he knew was his parents. He was pretty sure they'd kept their minds: two independent adults in the middle of the mentally dominated population of Santa Blanca.

They'd hidden that fact from everyone, even from him and Emma.

And when Ethan had discovered the Ch'zar and found out his parents might not be one of them, they vanished and left him a mysterious goodbye note . . . and a million unanswered questions.

Ethan sighed and kicked a stone.

He couldn't help Emma or his parents anymore. They were gone. The only thing he could do was help here and now—save the Resisters, fight, and keep his mind his own for as long as possible.

Paul marched up the dry riverbank and stopped.

Ethan, Felix, and Madison clambered up the slope after him. They stopped dead in their tracks.

It looked like a carnival had come to town.

The Ferris wheel spun, and neon flashed on its spokes. There were game booths with baseballs thrown at tin milk cans, coins tossed onto glass plates, and water pistols shot to fill balloons to the bursting point. There were rides, too: the Tilt-A-Whirl, Spin Out, and rattling roller coasters.

The lights and colors fascinated Ethan.

Apparently this wasn't a school night, because the kids here weren't doing their homework. They played the games and rode the rides.

But not like they were supposed to.

No one waited in line for the rides. They pushed and shoved their way to the front. And instead of playing the games by the rules, the kids cheated. Ethan couldn't believe it. They got way too close to throw for the baseball toss and even stole dimes from the coin toss!

None of the adults running the carnival seemed to care.

Paul kept his head down, let his hair fall into his eyes, and plodded ahead. "Come on. You haven't seen the half of it," he muttered.

They followed him around a corner.

Felix halted and whistled low.

Ahead was a street with wall-to-wall ice-cream parlors, pizza places, and candy stores. The smell was intoxicating: cheese and pepperoni and fresh crust, caramels, and melted milk chocolate.

Ethan's mouth watered.

Madison and Felix drifted closer to the food.

Felix's stomach grumbled so loudly that Ethan heard it four paces away.

Ethan couldn't remember how long it'd been since breakfast. The field protein bars in his pack tasted like sawdust (he suspected they *were* part sawdust).

He licked his lips. Maybe just one slice of pizza with extra pepperoni. How long would that take?

Paul stepped in front of them and shook his head.

"Don't," he said. "All the stuff here is meant to distract you. Take one bite and the next thing you know, you're eating all night."

Madison blinked rapidly as if she were waking from a dream.

Ethan squinted. Inside a pizza joint, the kids listened to music and danced—all while nonstop stuffing their faces with pizza.

Distract was an understatement.

"Heads up," Madison whispered. Her body tensed as she nodded down the street.

A gang of kids walked toward them. There were three boys and two girls. Most were older than them. One boy hefted a golf putter over his shoulder. One of the girls smoked a cigarette. Her brown hair had been clipped bowl-cut short.

Ethan recognized their purposeful stride and mean smiles. He'd seen this before on the soccer field, when the opposing team was up five points and they *still* drove toward the goal like it was a tie.

These kids were 100 percent trouble. They meant to crush their enemy.

The biggest boy in the pack looked over Ethan and the others. His gaze settled on Felix, who was still a head taller than him.

"What do we have here?" the kid said. He shifted the golf putter off his shoulder and *thunk*ed it into his hand.

Felix wasn't impressed. His eyes narrowed.

Ethan was sure Felix could knock this bully out with one punch.

"They're new kids," the smoking girl muttered around her cigarette. "Just look at their faces. So clueless." She blew smoke at Ethan and smiled at him, her black eyes glimmering with interest.

Ugh. The smoke stunk.

Ethan thought they had cured cigarettes decades ago. That must have been another lie told by the Ch'zar.

Madison bent her knees as if about to launch a vicious kick at the girl's head.

The combat training pounded into Ethan for the last month clicked into place. He recalled three things.

The first thing to remember in a fight: breathe.

He'd tensed up so much in those first practice fights that he'd forgotten to inhale. By the time Ethan had realized it, he was sucking wind.

The second thing to remember in a fight: a good stance.

Ethan shifted to get his feet solid under him. He bent his knees.

And the third thing to remember?

Don't fight more than one person at a time.

It was really, really hard.

Which is when Ethan noticed the Sterling kids had inched into a half circle around them.

"We're not new," Paul told them, and tilted his head to show off his scars. "We just got out late from Dorm H. We were just going to grab a bite."

"Bite?" The boy with the golf club snapped his teeth at Paul.

The other kids all laughed.

Sweat made Ethan's balled fists slippery as he braced for combat.

If Felix could drop two or three of them, they'd have a chance. As long as that one kid didn't start swinging that golf putter around like it was a Neanderthal club.

Ethan's pulse was a drumroll in his brain. The adrenaline in his blood made it hard to think about anything.

The other kids had them surrounded now.

Ethan went back-to-back with Paul and Felix. Madison scooted in beside him.

One sudden move would start this fight.

Before anyone took the first punch, though, a window on the third story of the billiard hall broke.

A flaming trash can pinwheeled from the window. It hit the ground, crumpled, and sent plumes of burning paper into the air.

"Fire toss contest!" the smoking girl said. Her face brightened. "Let's play. We can beat up freshmen anytime."

The boy in charge of the pack looked at the smoldering trash. "Yeah . . . let's go burn something."

He turned and he and his gang strode down the street.

The smoking girl looked over her shoulder at Ethan, winked, and said, "Catch you later. . . ."

"Too close," Paul whispered. "This way, before they change their minds." He ducked into a side street and quickly walked away.

"We would've pulverized them," Madison growled. "I am so going to knock that girl's head off next time I see her!"

"That's not why we're here," Felix said, clamping one massive hand on Madison's slender shoulder.

Ethan couldn't speak. He felt weak from the spent adrenaline. It was all he could do to shamble after Paul, who led them out onto another street with pinball arcades and soda bars. Most windows on the buildings here were busted. There were screams and laughs from inside.

This place was a nightmare.

They jogged up a set of concrete stairs and halted at a large iron gate. A high stone wall topped with barbed wire ran in either direction. On the gate was a polished silver S.

"Welcome to Sterling School for the Gifted," Paul said with a grimace. "If you thought it was weird and rough in Fiesta City, you haven't seen anything yet."

HOW NOT TO START
A SECRET MISSION

ETHAN, MADISON, AND FELIX FOLLOWED
Paul as he snuck onto the Sterling school grounds, slunk
between long shadows cast by oak trees, ran across a bed
of daisies, and then broke a window to get into a redbrick
building.

Inside, Paul paused. Moonlight spilled through the
windows onto a tile floor. There were canvas bins on
wheels.

"Laundry room," Paul whispered. He rummaged
through a bin and handed them black sweats. "These are
what everyone wears here."

Ethan changed out of his jeans and T-shirt and shucked on the sweats over his flight suit.

The sweats were stinky, but the fleece was comfortable and good camouflage at night.

Madison peered out the window. "Adults in the hall," she hissed. "Three with flashlights."

"All students are supposed to be in Fiesta City," Paul said. "We better lie low or we'll stick out."

They waited for the patrol of adults to pass, and then Paul led them across a grassy field. Sprinklers turned on with a *shunka-shunka-shunka*, and they sprinted ahead of the streams of water, almost getting soaked.

This place reminded Ethan of Northside Elementary back in Santa Blanca: P.E. fields, a building that had to be a cafeteria, based on the burned hamburger smell wafting from the place, classrooms with one wide wall of windows, covered walkways, and ivy on the brick walls. It seemed so normal, apart from the insane-asylum carnival that was Fiesta City and apart from the radioactive desert surrounding the place. Yeah, *totally* normal.

Paul halted at a metal door. "Dormitories," he said, and jimmied the lock. They slipped inside. Paul didn't turn on the lights.

As Ethan's eyes adjusted to the dark, he saw the room had two dozen empty cots. He sat on one that smelled of dust and didn't have a pillow or a blanket. "So we just wait here?"

It felt like the wrong thing to do. Ethan's instincts told him this was a dangerous place.

Felix flopped onto the stripped cot next to him and stretched. "Why not wait . . . just for a minute."

Madison sat, too, and yawned.

Ethan closed his eyes. The funny thing was, despite the excitement, the critical mission, the only thing he could think of was that he could really use a five-minute catnap.

He should be wide awake—thinking, searching, figuring out a way to find Sterling kids to recruit.

Instead, completely against his wishes, his head hit the mattress.

Alarm bells trilled and Ethan almost jumped out of his skin. His heart hammered in his chest as he sat up, fumbling through layers of panic to wakefulness.

Sunlight spilled in through the windows.

Ethan had fallen asleep? How'd he let *that* happen?

Madison, Paul, and Felix sat up in nearby cots.

There were twenty other kids in this room. They pulled pillows over their heads; some snored straight through the alarm. One boy tossed a book at the bell mounted on the wall and knocked it off.

A door slammed open and ten adults marched into the room. They wore black sweats like the rest of the kids but had a silver *S* embroidered on the chest.

"Get up!" the adults shouted. "Class in five minutes! Slackers, eat now or never!"

Ethan leaped to his feet.

One adult tossed a brown bag at Ethan, his friends, and the other kids who managed to get up. Inside the bag was an apple, a bacon-and-egg sandwich, and a carton of milk.

Most of the kids, though, kept sleeping.

The adults pulled out wooden batons. They smacked the sleeping kids, yanked off their blankets, and kicked them out of their cots.

"Late for class," one of the adults yelled, "and you run a *hundred* laps!"

Ethan's head cleared a little and he tasted a metal tang.

Knockout gas. He'd tasted the stuff before in the school bus that took him from Santa Blanca. The Ch'zar had tried to drug him into a deep sleep. That gas must be used to knock out the students here, which made sense, considering how insanely rowdy those kids in Fiesta City had been.

Ethan glanced at Felix.

Felix took a huge bite of his apple and nodded back, indicating they play along: they had to pretend to be Sterling students for now.

Great.

The last of the Sterling kids got up, complaining and grumbling. Ethan and his team marched into the hall and passed other kids filing out of dozens of other dormitories.

They got pushed farther down the hall, then outside into a covered walkway. That led into another building, where they were shoved into a classroom.

The room was full of blackboards and desks and tables with miniature three-dimensional landscapes on them. They reminded Ethan of a model train setup—only these landscapes had gridlines. In the corners were miniature soldiers with muskets and swords, tiny cannons, and men mounted on horseback.

On the blackboard were the words:

TACTICS 101

Scrawled underneath were rules explaining how the soldiers moved, attacked, and defended, and who won when they fought.

Ethan was intrigued. This didn't look so bad, almost like a normal classroom. He might even learn something here.

"It's just a game?" Madison asked, and she scratched her head under her baseball cap.

"Keep your caps on," Paul whispered. "If the teachers see your faces, they may recognize you—and we'll be cooked."

Ethan pulled his cap down so low he could barely see past the brim.

Every adult here was part of the Ch'zar collective hive mind. They'd know Ethan Blackwood—the kid who'd blown up the Geo Transit Tunnel, fought the Battle of Northside Elementary, and then escaped their perfect neighborhood to join the Resisters.

A teacher with black-rimmed glasses entered and announced, "Pair off and play, kids."

One girl challenged Felix to a match. Felix looked at his friends, shrugged, and set up the pieces on a table.

"Don't be such a dork." Paul shouldered past Ethan. "Blend in, Blackwood."

Paul nodded at Madison and they grabbed a table.

Ethan shuffled into the corner, far from the gaze of that teacher. There was a boy there who had more muscles on one arm than Ethan had in his entire body. One front tooth was chipped.

"I'll take red," the muscle-bound boy told him with a growl. "You take the green pieces."

Ethan read the rules on the blackboard. He saw how a defense and an offense could be built, taking advantage of the units' abilities and overlapping ranges of weapons.

Kid stuff.

"Sure," Ethan told the boy. "Whatever."

His opponent moved first into the middle of the board.

Ethan studied the terrain. You didn't worry about the ground when you flew an I.C.E. suit or played on a soccer field. In this game, though, he somehow knew it was vital.

He sent his cavalry to engage the other boy's frontline soldiers and lured them back.

His opponent chased but struggled up a hillside just to get pounded to smithereens by Ethan's cannons. Ethan moved his infantry to mop up the survivors.

In three minutes he'd cleared the board. Ethan hadn't lost a single piece.

"You . . . you can't do that," the other boy stammered, and smashed his fist on the table, sending the pieces flying.

A few students came over, interested in the massacre of a game.

One boy with dark skin, ice-blue eyes, and a look of intense concentration pushed the muscled kid away. "Don't worry, Kris," he said. "I'll play him next."

The big kid looked relieved. "This'll be good," he said with a chuckle.

Ethan had a bad feeling about this—especially when *more* kids gathered around the table to watch. One was the girl from last night, the one with the bobbed hair, the one in the gang who'd threatened them. Today she chewed gum and watched intently as Ethan set up his pieces.

What if the teacher noticed him?

Ethan pulled his cap down even tighter and focused on the game, hoping he could somehow become invisible.

° ° ° 15 ° ° °

SURFING FOR AGGRESSION

ETHAN BRIEFLY CONSIDERED LOSING. THAT would attract less attention.

But he *wanted* to win. Maybe it was too much time logged in his Infiltrator I.C.E. suit, too much time in contact with the wasp's brain, but a part of him *couldn't* give up. Even if it was a game. Even with so much more at stake if he got discovered.

So . . . he compromised.

For this game, Ethan didn't use the horsemen lure trick. Instead he ran his cavalry behind his opponent and attacked from the rear. Meanwhile, Ethan's foot soldiers, protecting his cannons, mounted the high ground and pounded his enemy's weakened defenses.

It wasn't perfect. He lost half of his cavalry. Ethan did, though, *crush* his opponent.

The dark-skinned boy raised an eyebrow. "You're really good," he whispered with genuine appreciation. "I'm Oliver. What was your name again?"

"Uh . . . Ethan," Ethan whispered.

The girl with the short hair stopped chewing her gum and mouthed his name as if considering if it was a good or bad thing.

The teacher moved over and leafed through an attendance list.

Ethan ducked his head.

Madison pushed her way over. "Nice 'blending in,'" she said.

Why had he won so blatantly? To show these Sterling kids he was better?

Now the teacher was about to figure out Ethan didn't belong here.

The classroom bell jangled. Ethan jumped.

The kids abandoned their games and marched into the hallway and then outside.

Ethan hurriedly went out with them before that

teacher realized he wasn't supposed to be there. He exhaled a huge sigh of relief as he left the tactics class.

That had been superclose.

He caught up to Madison and the others to apologize, but then almost stumbled over his own feet as he spotted a *new* problem.

Two robotic suits marched on the edge of the grassy playground. They were like the athletic suits Ethan had piloted in soccer—twelve feet tall and six hundred pounds of stainless steel, hydraulically powered, skeletal frame.

These had adult pilots, though.

Instead of orange gecko-gripped feet and palms to handle soccer balls, these suits had shoulder mounted cannons and carried lances that crackled with electricity.

These were meant for battle.

Evading adult teachers in a classroom was one thing. But guards in cybernetic suits? They'd be impossible to fight or outrun.

He'd have to be extra careful.

They filed into the next classroom. It was a chemistry lab.

It was actually more like the *opposite* of a chemistry class. In every chem class Ethan had ever taken, the teacher had stressed "safety first." In this class, though, the

Sterling teacher taught his students the best way to burn and blow things up.

Ethan scooted to the back of the room as the teacher demonstrated how to mix chemicals that boiled and frothed and shattered a glass beaker.

Felix nodded to the corner and the Resisters drifted to the pencil sharpener and pretended to use it.

"This is nuts," Madison whispered.

"Did you see in tactics class?" Felix asked, and stared at Ethan. "The teacher took notes on everyone winning that game."

Ethan flushed. "It wasn't my fault. I was just playing smart."

That sounded foolish even to his own ears.

Madison's and Paul's write-up of his flight performance was still bothering him. Did he *have to* win every battle? Even if doing so made him lose the war? That might be the literal truth if he drew too much attention to himself here at Sterling.

"It wasn't just you." Felix looked around to see if anyone was listening.

The other kids were busy practicing the blowing-up-the-beaker experiment (most not even using protective eyewear).

"The teacher was assessing all the winners," Felix continued, his large brow wrinkled with concern. "They're sorting for talent. Or in this case, for aggression."

"But why?" Madison turned her sharp eyes to Paul for answers.

Paul didn't meet her gaze. "Don't ask me," he said. "I got out of this place before they singled me out for 'bad behavior.' Look, forget about what they're doing here and let's do some 'selecting' of our own and get a few kids back to base."

Ethan was dying to know exactly how Paul escaped this place the first time.

An even better question was *why* did Paul leave? He had an attitude problem, he was a bully, and he had a total disregard for authority. He was a perfect fit for Sterling.

Maybe there was more to Paul Hicks's story than simply walking away. Ethan bet there was also more to Paul *coming back* than to rescue a few kids for the Resistance.

"What are you suggesting?" Ethan asked.

"We need to get to a computer," Paul whispered. "Then we can access the student records. We can sort through the ones that . . . I don't know . . . the ones that even the Ch'zar think are too much trouble."

There was more. Ethan could feel it. Paul was holding back something big.

"That's a good plan," Felix said. "We'll do it after classes, before they let everyone loose into Fiesta City tonight."

"Wait," Paul said. "It's Tuesday, right? That's a P.E. day." His head snapped up. "We can't wait. We've got to get out. Right *now*. Steal some bathroom passes or—"

The classroom bell trilled.

"That's it!" the chem teacher shouted, and moved to get a fire extinguisher. "*Don't* clean up. Leave your experiments. Move on to your next class."

Against their will, they got herded into the hallway and then outside.

Five guards in athletic suits marched alongside them, escorting them to the grassy physical education field.

"Great," Madison said. "So we play a little soccer or baseball." She cracked her knuckles. "We'll wipe the ground with these punks."

Teachers handed out sticks.

Ethan took one. It was five feet long and lightly padded. Field hockey? He hefted it. They were too heavy for that.

The Sterling kids warmed up, twirling the sticks so fast they whistled through the air.

More kids poured onto the field, spreading out so they were evenly spaced across the entire playground.

"Keep close," Paul whispered to them, deadly serious.

"What's going on?" Ethan asked, suddenly feeling something was very wrong.

He got his answer as a P.E. coach shouted, "Okay, kids, ready, set"—he blew a whistle—"FIGHT!"

∘ ∘ ∘ 16 ∘ ∘ ∘

BATTLE CLASS

EVERY KID ON THE FIELD SCREAMED AND attacked one another.

They jabbed sticks into faces, groins, and stomachs.

It was like the battles Ethan had just seen in Tactics 101. Only instead of miniature soldiers on a table with gridlines and rules, there were a hundred crazed students swinging sticks—totally insane!

Half the kids went down within seconds. Dozens of students lay crumpled, groaning and crying.

Ethan felt the air move by his head. He ducked. A stick narrowly missed cracking his skull.

He turned. It was a boy almost as big as Felix, the

leader of the gang who had wanted to beat the Resisters up last night in Fiesta City.

Ethan had fought lots of times in an I.C.E. battle suit, in matches during Resister boot camp, but never with his bare fists or with a stick.

Everything that had been drilled and beaten into him in boot camp came flooding back: breathe, get a good stance, and . . . well, forget that last part about trying to fight one person at a time.

He sidestepped as three kids crashed between Ethan and the gang leader. The three fell in a heap and wrestled on the grass.

Ethan, meanwhile, used that distraction.

He swung high at his opponent.

The other boy blocked, flipped his stick around, and smashed it at Ethan's ribs.

Ethan blocked—barely.

The impact shuddered up his stick and numbed his arm. If it *had* connected, padding or not, it would have broken Ethan's bones.

Were they crazy? Did the Sterling teachers want these kids to seriously hurt each other? That made no sense, even for the Ch'zar.

He'd figure out why later. First he had to *survive* this class.

He couldn't be scared. He had to fight.

Ethan borrowed a tactic he'd learned battling in an I.C.E. suit. When ranged weapons didn't work, you had to get in close to rip your enemy apart.

He moved toward the bigger boy, got so near neither could swing, and Ethan socked him in the nose.

"Ow!" The boy dropped to one knee, let go of his stick, and held his face. "You hit me with your *hand*! You're supposed to use your stick, idiot! There are rules!"

Ethan wasn't interested in following the rules of *this* game, especially if that meant getting clobbered.

But he hesitated and couldn't bring himself to hit the boy again.

This wasn't a fight-to-the-death real battle with the Ch'zar.

The bigger kid who'd tried to break his ribs a second ago was still human, maybe even someone Ethan could save and recruit into the Resistance.

The boy started to get to his feet. He grabbed his stick, laughing.

Madison ran to Ethan and kicked the boy over. She stabbed him once, hard, in the back of the knee.

The boy screamed and went down.

"You *want* to be hit?" she growled at Ethan. "Get your head in the game, Blackwood!"

Ethan blinked. He looked around.

Felix was ten paces from them and surrounded. He beat back five other kids. One got behind him and jabbed Felix in the kidney. He grunted and fell like a huge redwood, trying to clutch at the pain in his back.

Ethan and Madison were on those kids in an instant—punching, kicking, and clubbing them off their friend.

Paul appeared to protect their backs.

The field fell quiet.

There were just twenty kids left standing. They panted, nursed bruised hands, and tensed to spring. They were the meanest, toughest, and the best fighters at Sterling . . . and they all searched one another for any sign of weakness.

One of them pointed at Ethan and his friends. "Hey! No teaming up!"

"Why don't you come over and try to stop us?" Ethan shouted back.

Madison groaned and rolled her eyes.

Ethan instantly regretted saying that, because the remaining kids did just that. They circled them and stepped closer and closer.

Felix got up, grimacing with pain. He gripped his padded hockey stick so hard the wood crackled.

Ethan had never seen Felix mad before, but now he

sensed cold anger radiating from him in waves. Like his mother.

"Let's finish this," Felix said.

The other kids stopped in their tracks, calculating the odds of taking on the four of them (now with the addition of the much larger Felix to their group).

They charged.

Felix swept aside the first two in a single blow. Madison jabbed and poked the soft spots in her opponents. Paul calmly whirled his stick around like an expert martial artist.

There were so many students rushing them at once that Ethan managed to connect with only one boy—and got his hands clobbered from the return blow for his trouble.

He almost dropped his stick it hurt so much.

He was wide open as the kid facing him reared back to smack him.

Out of nowhere, a girl jumped at this opponent, swung, and connected with the side of the kid's head.

The boy about to clobber Ethan dropped to the ground, knocked out cold.

The girl winked at Ethan, then spun, her bowl-cut hair *whoosh*ing around her, and hit the other kids, screaming like she was nuts (or totally having fun).

It was the girl in the gang from last night. The same one who'd apparently taken an interest in Ethan in tactics class.

A whistle blew and three teachers marched onto the grassy field, jotting notes on their clipboards.

All the kids stopped fighting.

Ethan sucked wind.

He'd forgotten to breathe.

He got his bearings. His friends were okay . . . well, at least standing.

The other side? Only four other kids were up. Two he didn't know, the girl who'd saved him, and the kid with dark skin who'd challenged Ethan earlier in tactics class.

"That's enough!" One teacher came over to Ethan. "There are no teams. That's a violation of Sterling rules."

Rules? Rules at Sterling was like giving a person stranded on a desert island an Arctic survival parka.

Paul stepped in front of Ethan before he could protest. His cap was pulled low, and he looked away as he spoke to the teacher. "Sorry about that, Coach. It just kind of happened."

The teacher examined the carnage around them, nodding in approval as kids limped off the field. "Nice work, but I want you all to report for evaluation."

Evaluation? Ethan wasn't sure what that was, but he didn't like the sound of it. *Anything* that got them more noticed by the teachers and those guards in athletic suits was bad news.

"Evaluation," the teacher continued, "for *disciplinary action*."

DO I KNOW YOU?

THEY WERE DOOMED. THERE WAS NO WAY TO get out of this.

If it'd just been the one teacher from the field walking them to this "evaluation," then they could have made a break for it. Ethan and his companions, though, had picked up an escort of two athletic-suited guards as well.

Ethan knew the specs on the athletic suits he'd used in soccer. They ran as fast as a car and could lift two tons with one arm—not to mention, these Sterling models had shoulder-mounted cannons and electrified lances.

He imagined trying to make a break for it—him and his friends scattering. Maybe *one* of them could get away.

Could one or two of them reach their I.C.E. suits in time to save the others?

He wasn't sure.

He didn't try it. Not yet.

The teacher marched them into the school, through the front office where teachers filled out forms or made phone calls, and then they stopped at a door marked PRINCIPAL KENDELL.

The P.E. teacher knocked. There was a muffled voice from the other side, and then the teacher pushed open the door for them.

Paul looked like he was going to throw up, and cast around looking for a way out. There was none.

They shuffled inside.

Principal Kendell sat at her desk typing on her computer and shuffling through a pile of paperwork. She reminded Ethan of his mom, with her golden skin, intelligent eyes, and an easy smile. She wore a navy blue jacket with a silver *S* on the vest pocket.

The one window in her office had curtains drawn back and blinds up to let the sunlight spill inside. Diplomas and awards hung on the walls.

This was part of the huge lie.

This principal had never gotten any awards. She didn't have to fill out paperwork when she had a direct mental link with the Ch'zar mind-controlled Collective.

It made Ethan angry, because he'd lived the same lie in Santa Blanca for most of his life. But he kept that anger in check because of another emotion flooding through him: fear.

The Ch'zar were about to discover him and his friends.

The principal looked up from her computer.

The P.E. teacher handed her a clipboard. "Rule violators, Madam Principal," he said.

She glanced at the clipboard. "That will be all, Coach," she told him. "I'll see to their evaluation."

The coach grunted, left, and shut the door behind him.

Ethan tilted his head and looked at the floor. Fear thundered through his brain and made it near impossible to think.

This wasn't the first time he'd been called in for disciplinary action. He'd been in Coach Norman's office back at Northside Elementary for a Ch'zar interrogation. He'd been chewed out by Colonel Winter, not once, but *twice*, in her office.

But this time was very different.

One good look at any of their faces and the principal

would recognize them, or at least recognize they weren't supposed to be at Sterling.

They'd be captured and jailed until they reached puberty.

Then the Ch'zar would really have them. Their minds would be absorbed into the Collective.

Paul, Felix, Madison, and Ethan would cease to be themselves.

Principal Kendell read the report and made tsking sounds. "The rules of our program were explained on your first day," she said. "There are *no* teams. Physical education is to assess your *individual* potentials."

Despite their dire situation, Ethan was curious. Why test individuals when the Ch'zar were going to absorb every Sterling kid into their Collective? Weren't they all supposed to work together to strip-mine the world and build starships?

Felix elbowed Ethan. He narrowed his eyes and shot Ethan that "we have to accomplish our mission at any cost" look. He then nodded at the principal.

Ethan understood.

They had to do something about her, quick, before she realized who they really were. Ethan, though, had no idea what exactly they *could* do.

The principal set down the clipboard, stood, and

walked toward them. "This is a serious infraction," she said. "But relax. I'll make a show of it for the coach, give you a few demerits, and call it even . . . *if* you each promise to play the game by the rules."

As she passed in front of Ethan, he glued his gaze to the floor.

She sounded so nice.

For a split second, Ethan believed she might be a *real* principal. But that was just his Santa Blanca upbringing, his brainwashed reaction to authority making him doubt the truth . . . and himself.

Felix cleared his throat.

The principal turned to him.

What was he doing?

"Yes, um, Mr. . . . ?" The principal reached back for the clipboard and scanned it. "That's strange. Coach didn't write down your names."

Ethan then understood: Felix had distracted her so Ethan could make his move.

It was now or never.

He had to do *something* . . . anything.

Ethan spied a paperweight on her desk. It was glass, had a sunflower inside, and was the size of his fist. He grabbed it. It was heavy—just the thing to conk someone on the back of the head.

He raised the paperweight but froze.

He couldn't.

Even with all his new hand-to-hand combat training, Ethan just didn't have it in him to hit someone with their back turned.

Sure, Ethan had fought the Ch'zar before, but in the air, with them shooting lasers and missiles at him. He'd even kicked one of their human operatives in the face: Coach Norman back at Northside Elementary when he was about to drug Ethan.

He raised the paperweight higher.

But Principal Kendell seemed normal. She reminded Ethan of his mom.

Besides, he might really hurt her.

He exhaled. There was no way he could do this.

The principal whirled around, glanced at the paper-weight in his hand, and then her eyes fixed on Ethan's face.

Something focused in her gaze . . . and then faded as if she stared off into the distance. "Do I know you?" she whispered.

° ° ° 18 ° ° °

KIDS LIKE US

MADISON MOVED WITH THE SPEED OF A panther. She ripped a plaque for Principal of the Year off the wall, gritted her teeth, and smacked it over Principal Kendell's head.

With a crack of wood, the principal slumped and dropped to the floor, unconscious.

"Are you *trying* to get us killed?" Madison demanded of Ethan. "She almost recognized you!"

He stood and stared, stunned.

That had been the right thing to do. The principal

wasn't a real person. She was part of the Ch'zar Collective. Something entirely alien.

But his parents were adults and somehow outside the power of the Collective. More important, part of the principal *had to be* human . . . because if she wasn't, there was no hope for *any* of the kids who became adults. There'd be no hope for his sister Emma.

Felix knelt and felt for the principal's pulse.

"She's okay. Just knocked out." Felix glanced at the closed office door. "If she didn't recognize you, Ethan, we've got a minute or two before someone comes."

Madison moved to the window and snapped shut the blinds. "Just perfect," she muttered.

Paul sat at the principal's desk and rapid-fire tapped on her computer keyboard.

"What are you doing?" Ethan moved behind Paul to get a better look.

Paul opened up student files and searched with a determination that made Ethan think Paul was looking for a *specific* someone.

Ethan spun the chair around. "Spill it," he told Paul. "You've been hiding something about this place."

"There's no time." Paul strained back toward the computer.

Ethan knew he was right about Paul having some big secret.

"Make time," Ethan demanded. "You're terrified of this place. That much is obvious, and I don't blame you. You came back, though. I think to help us out, but there's more to it than that. What?"

Madison and Felix exchanged appraising looks. They moved closer, curious what Paul was doing on the computer, too.

"Okay." Paul's face scrunched with irritation, and it made the scars on his cheek pucker. "Just let me work while I tell you. But then"—his voice lowered to a threatening whisper—"don't blame me if you all end up wishing I'd kept my mouth shut."

Ethan felt as if Paul had punched him in the nose. He let go of the chair.

Paul went back to his search, opening one student record after another.

"When I was here," Paul explained, "I was the worst of these punks. I beat up the new kids; ate all the junk food; broke, burned, and blew up things. I ran with three of my best buddies and one little kid, Jeff. He was like our mascot."

Paul hesitated, and then went on. "We even broke

Sterling's rules. We didn't care. One night instead of going into Fiesta City, we snuck into the place where they 'graduated' students."

A cold feeling spread through Ethan.

He'd been told that when he graduated, he'd go to high school. Ethan had studied extra hard to get into the best schools. In reality, though, he would have been taken away to join the Ch'zar Collective.

"I had friends graduate, too," he said consolingly.

"Not like this," Paul said. "The way they graduate people *here* . . . it's why they select the aggressive ones. Why they weed out the kids with independent streaks." Paul looked at Ethan, and Felix, and then Madison, unable to say more.

A chill shuddered down Madison's back and she took a step back.

"Don't you get it?" Paul managed to say in a strangled whisper. "The most aggressive and independent kids don't *just* get absorbed into the hive mind. They stick them into I.C.E. suits."

Ethan had heard Paul perfectly, but his words didn't make sense and felt like they bounced and tumbled through his brain. "I.C.E. suits?" he echoed.

"That's not possible . . . ," Madison said.

"We *saw* it," Paul said. "The giant bugs . . . a bunch of

kids going willingly inside . . . technicians riveting them into the suit. *Permanently*. They were just like us. Only a little older." His eyes narrowed and blinked and brimmed with tears.

"That's who we've been fighting all this time," Paul whispered. "Kids like us. Maybe not in every Ch'zar I.C.E. suit, but there are smart ones, leaders in a swarm. Those are different than the others . . . because they're piloted."

Ethan got it. In the simulations, he'd seen how some enemy units were special.

The other wasps, the locusts, the beetles he'd fought and killed in Santa Blanca, even those black widow spiders that had tried to murder Paul—they could've had *humans* inside them.

He felt sick. He sucked in a deep breath, but that didn't help.

Human kids were trying to kill them—sure, they were all mind-controlled, but they were human nonetheless.

He wanted to tell Paul he was a liar.

But one more thing about it made some sense.

Dr. Irving said the Resistance had borrowed the I.C.E. technology from the Ch'zar. The fighting suit cockpits, the controls, all that stuff had *already* been engineered by the aliens . . . because they had pilots inside them, too.

It changed everything.

How could Ethan fight them knowing that inside the Ch'zar armor might be his old friends—even his sister Emma?

"They caught us," Paul went on. "We'd seen the truth. We didn't have a clue *what* we'd actually seen, but they couldn't put us back with the rest of the Sterling kids. So they have this place here, Ward Zero, where they isolate kids who've seen things. They tell everyone else that they're crazy."

"That's when you escaped?" Felix asked.

"I ran. Got out of here," Paul said. "I would've rather died in the desert than stay. But the colonel found me. . . ." Paul exhaled and his attention snapped back to the computer.

On-screen flashed new student records, each with a big red WARD ZERO PATIENT.

Paul tabbed through the files.

"My friends aren't here," he whispered. "I'm too late." Paul pounded the desk with his fist.

Ethan wanted to tell Paul he was sorry, that he knew what it felt like to lose someone you cared about to the Ch'zar.

Something more important, something *impossible*, caught his eye, though.

"Go back! Back!" Ethan told him.

Paul called up the last file.

On the computer was the name of a Ward Zero patient that made Ethan's heart pound with joy, hope, and then dread:

BLACKWOOD, EMMA KATHERINE.

∘ ∘ ∘ 19 ∘ ∘ ∘

WARD ZERO

ETHAN WENT OUT THE WINDOW OF THE PRIN-
cipal's office.

There was no time to come up with an airtight plan.
Ethan's sister was here.

He'd thought he'd lost her forever.

Emma had always gotten Ethan into trouble, and
they'd always argued, but she was also the only one who'd
stuck by him when the other neighborhood kids teased
him about coming from a small family.

Emma was a year older than Ethan. That meant she

could hit puberty at *any time*. She could get absorbed into the Collective today!

If there was any chance she was still human, he had to get her out of here.

One more reason to hurry: Even if Principal Kendell hadn't recognized Ethan's face, someone was bound to check on her soon. Then every adult, every enemy I.C.E. fighting suit circling Fiesta City would come for them.

Ethan dropped from the window ledge to the ground. He crouched behind a juniper hedge.

Two adults in cybernetic athletic suits patrolled the freshly cut lawn between the administration building and the dormitories. The heavy steel frames made the ground tremble as they passed.

Madison landed next to Ethan.

Felix dropped with a thud after her. He crouched on all fours behind the hedge.

Paul eased out the window next and slid it shut behind him.

"Those guards are still patrolling," Felix whispered, "not searching for us or running for the office. That means they still don't know anything. So we just walk out of here—pretend we're four kids late for class."

"Then we better hurry," Ethan said, "because *that* won't last long."

He gathered his courage and strode onto the lawn, walking past one of the hulking athletic suits. Its shoulder-mounted cannon looked big enough to take on an I.C.E. suit.

Ethan's heart hammered in his chest. It took all his willpower *not* to run.

The adults in six hundred pounds of hydraulics, armor plate, and weapons clanked by, eyeing Ethan suspiciously but otherwise trudging along in a straight line.

Madison, Felix, and Paul caught up.

"You *are* crazy," Paul said with a snort. "I'm beginning to like that about you." He darted down a walkway. "This way." He broke into a trot, and then a full sprint.

Paul led them to a part of the school that had chain-link fences topped with razor wire. There were signs on the fence showing stick figures zapped by lightning. There were no students or teachers anywhere in sight.

Ethan tensed, waiting for alarms.

The teachers, though, could communicate silently. Telepathically. They could signal each other to release sleep gas into the corridors.

Ethan and his team could just wake up, captured . . . or not wake up at all.

Paul skidded to a halt before a rusty gate with a pad-lock. It was plastered with more electrocution warnings and NO TRESPASSING signs.

Madison dug into her sweats, grabbed the flight suit gloves tucked under her belt, and snapped them on. From a tiny pocket on her flight suit, she took out a tool kit and pulled out two metal picks.

"Don't touch it," Ethan told her. "It's electrif—"

She knelt and picked the padlock.

"Her gloves are insulated," Felix told Ethan. "This isn't the first time we've broken into a place the Ch'zar have locked up."

The padlock clicked open. Madison cracked a wry, crooked smile and slipped through the gate.

She came back a second later and whispered, "Coast is clear."

Beyond was a small hospital made of white brick. A sign on the dead lawn surrounding it read:

WARD ZERO. RESTRICTED ACCESS.

VISITORS BY APPOINTMENT ONLY.

Ethan scoffed. More lies.

Like the kids inside ever got visitors . . . except when the Ch'zar came for them.

"There's a skylight," Paul said. "That's how I busted out the first time. We can get in that way, too, and avoid the staff."

They snuck around back.

Madison pointed to a gutter pipe running along the wall. She clambered up the pipe and onto the roof like a spider monkey.

Paul followed with a practiced ease.

Ethan went next, grunting with effort, and for one insane moment, he wished he'd had *more* physical training in boot camp.

Felix came up last, slow but sure.

The pipe groaned and pulled away from the wall. He froze.

After a heart-pounding second, though, the pipe settled, and Felix inched up the rest of the way.

They all sighed.

Paul and Ethan then jimmied open the skylight. They all dropped down, snuck along a green-tiled hallway with flickering fluorescent lights, and came to a corridor that had doors numbered 1 through 20.

Paul traced the number 3 on one door.

"This was my friend Jeff's room," he said, and bit his lip. "I should have taken him with me. I should have taken them all. I was so scared. Once I found a way out through that skylight, I just ran for it."

Ethan knew how Paul had felt.

It'd been like that the first time he'd seen the Ch'zar's giant insects. He'd just wanted to bolt like a scared animal.

Paul opened the door.

The room had two cots, linens stacked neatly on their ends. It was empty.

Paul's shoulders slumped.

The door to the adjacent room opened. A boy younger than Ethan came out in a blue hospital gown and slippers. He looked half asleep. "Are you new?" he asked them.

"There was a kid who used to be in this room," Paul said, his voice cracking with emotion. "Where is he?"

The other boy shook his head. "Jeff, yeah, I remember. They took him away. . . ."

Paul swallowed hard. His jaw clenched with rage.

"I'm sorry," Ethan whispered to Paul. "We got a mission to do, though. We can still save the rest of them."

Paul looked at Ethan like he'd spoken in a foreign language; then he glanced down the hall.

"Are there others here?" Paul asked the kid in the hospital gown.

The boy nodded, sensing now that something was

very different about them. He went from door to door, knocking.

An older girl stepped from room 11. She was tall and athletic, and had cinched her hospital gown about her waist with string to make it look more like a white dress. Her long black hair was intricately braided, and freckles splashed over her golden skin.

Ethan blinked, not quite believing what he saw.

"Emma?" he cried.

She blinked, too. She stared at Ethan—then grinned and ran and crashed into him, hugging him so hard he could barely breathe.

He hugged her back.

She was solid, not just his imagination.

Emma was the only part of his old life left in the entire world. He hadn't realized how much he'd needed that. He'd never known how much he cared for his sister until he'd lost her . . . and then got her back—his teasing, practical-joking, punching-him-in-the-arm older sister. For a second he felt like a little kid again, like his older sister was going to take care of him like she always had.

"I thought you were gone for good," Ethan whispered. "Last time I saw you, they were dragging you onto that zeppelin."

Emma pushed him away. Her smile faded.

"You *were* there." She wiped away tears of joy, and her eyes narrowed with suspicion. "Those bugs. You're one of them!"

"It's not like that." Ethan held up his hands. "I mean, yes, I was in an Infiltrator wasp, but"—he waved his hands around the room—"I'm not part of any of *this*."

Ethan had started a battle that had raged through Northside Elementary in an attempt to rescue Emma. Resisters and Ch'zar had fought each other in their I.C.E. suits—giant monsters that had destroyed the entire school.

Emma had spotted him, he remembered. Somehow she'd recognized something familiar about his wasp.

Ethan had no idea *how* she'd known it was him inside, though.

A half-dozen other kids in pajamas emerged from their rooms. They all had dull, hopeless expressions—but they lit up with curiosity as they took in Ethan and the others.

"Maybe some of you have seen the truth—the giant bugs," Ethan told them. "We're part of a resistance fighting them with our own type of insects. We have to. The adults can't help us. They're all mind-controlled by the Ch'zar."

Everyone looked confused.

Ethan realized how crazy he must sound.

"Ch'zar?" Emma asked, her eyes darting from Ethan to his friends. She took a step away from them.

Felix stepped up. "The Ch'zar are aliens," he told her. "They came to Earth fifty years ago and conquered the world with their mind-control powers, but it only works on adults."

Emma listened. Her dark, narrowed eyes eased a fraction as she warily looked Felix over.

"So they created the neighborhoods," Madison added, "to raise every kid to the peak of their physical and mental potential, until they grew up and could be absorbed. It's totally evil."

Paul glanced into vacant room 3, hesitated, then seemed to decide something and stepped forward to stand with his fellow Resisters.

"We came to break you out," Paul told them. "We want you to help us fight the Ch'zar."

The other kids stared at them, stunned.

Having your entire reality turned upside down in a few minutes was a lot to take in.

But they *had* to believe, at least part of their story. These Ward Zero kids got put here because they'd all seen something the Ch'zar hadn't wanted them to see.

They needed more than understanding, though.

They needed a reason to fight.

"It's not just your life and minds at stake," Ethan told them. "We're fighting to save the entire world. We're fighting so no more kids have to go through what we've been through."

The first boy in the blue hospital gown seemed to wake up. Even though he was the smallest among them, he stood as tall as he could. "My name is Carl," he said. "I'll go! I'll fight!"

The other kids, though, looked even *more* scared than before. They bolted back into their rooms and slammed their doors.

Emma took a tentative step closer to Ethan, still looking at him funny. She smoothed a hand over her long braid, thinking.

"It's so strange," she whispered. "I know what you're saying is true. The things I saw that night, and Mom and Dad. They were different from the others—"

Ethan gave her a slight shake of his head, and Emma stopped.

He wasn't ready to share that part of his story with the others.

She seemed to understand.

How would the Resistance react to finding out his mom and dad weren't under the *complete* mental domination of the Ch'zar?

Would they suspect there was something different about Ethan and Emma, too? Take them out of the fight? Study their brains?

"We definitely need to talk about Mom and Dad," he said to her, "but later."

One kid who had retreated into her room bolted back into the hallway. She pointed behind her, trying to say something, but she was so panicked she couldn't get the words out.

Ethan stepped into her room.

There was nothing but two cots, a washbasin, and a window.

He looked outside. Beyond the bars and the wire safety glass was a view of the Ward Zero courtyard and the elec-trified gates—where athletic-suited guards clanked over cobblestones and rosebushes and surrounded the hospital.

∘ ∘ ∘ 20 ∘ ∘ ∘

ESCAPE . . . ALMOST

NUMBNESS SPREAD THROUGH ETHAN. IT started in his fingers and toes and oozed up his spine into his head. It was a *total* fear lockdown.

He'd never faced enemies in suits like these before without a suit of his own, but the old soccer training nonetheless clicked on.

He snapped out of his terrified state and his mind raced.

There were enough athletic suits down there with shoulder cannons and electrified lances to run down and crush a hundred unsuited kids. But there was *always* a way through the opposition's defense to the goal. This time, though, victory wouldn't be kicking a ball into a net. It would be getting out of Ward Zero alive.

One guard looked up at Ethan. Targeting laser sights flashed.

He backed up . . . into Madison, who stood behind him, gazing over his shoulder, her normally cute features scrunched in pure battle concentration.

"Those things," Emma said, her eyes widening, "they take the kids away." She whirled toward Ethan. "We have to save everyone here."

"This isn't a rescue mission anymore," Paul said, his voice edged with anger and disappointment. "We came to *recruit* kids like us who want to fight—not wimps! We have to get out while we still can."

Ethan couldn't accept that. He stepped into the hall.

"We can fight them!" he shouted at the shut doors. "Come with us! If we work together, we can get out of this mess."

The girl whose room they were in shook her head and ran off.

But another boy emerged. He was hopping into a pair of jeans. His jet-black hair stood up like a dandelion from static electricity. He stood next to Emma and Carl, who were still in their hospital gowns.

"I'm Lee," he said. "I want to go with you. I don't care where—as long as it's away from this place!"

"Good," Ethan said.

"I'm going to talk to the rest of them," Emma said, casting a lethal glare at Paul. "We *can* save them." She moved to a shut door.

An explosion rocked the building.

"They're coming," Felix said, and set one hand gently on Emma's arm.

Emma hesitated.

Thunder rolled into the hospital. The safety glass windows cracked.

Ethan stared at the shut doors. He wanted to save the rest of the Ward Zero kids, too, but there was no time left.

They'd persuaded just three kids to come. It wasn't the dozens of pilot recruits Ethan had imagined he'd be rescuing from Sterling, but it was a start.

If they escaped.

Ethan had to think fast. What advantage *did* they have over the Ch'zar-controlled adults outside?

He and his friends were better motivated, that was for sure. And unlike the Ch'zar, who made up their minds and stuck to it, Ethan could be unpredictable.

"I've got a plan," Ethan said.

Doubt crushed onto his shoulders like a three-ton weight. His friends huddled around him, though. They looked to him because Ethan knew how to get into and then *out* of trouble—at least that's what Madison, Felix, and even Paul seemed to believe as they stared at him.

Downstairs, glass shattered and heavy mechanical steps shook the walls.

Emma stepped closer to Ethan. She trembled, but she was still here, still standing by her brother.

"We backtrack to the skylight and get out that way," Ethan told them. "There will only be a moment to see everything from the roof and then we'll be spotted. We'll use that to our advantage and send our fastest runner to one corner to distract the enemy. The others will go down the rainspout on the other side."

"Genius plan," Paul muttered. "Who's nominated as 'fastest runner'?"

"Me," Ethan said. "I wouldn't ask anyone else."

"No way," Madison protested.

Emma looked at Madison and then at Ethan. She arched one eyebrow and cocked her head at Ethan as if to say "girlfriend"?

"No time to argue about it," Ethan told them, not answering his sister. "I can outthink those guards. Easy.

But we'll then need to find another way to get back to the main campus."

"There's a service entrance for food and trash," Emma told him. "It's locked, though."

"Probably electrified, too," Madison said. "I'll get us through that."

"Once back in the school, we'll lie low until classes let out," Ethan continued, "and slip into Fiesta City tonight. From there it'll be a short way back to the I.C.E. suits."

Ethan didn't dare show a shred of doubt, even though there was nothing *but* doubt boiling in his stomach. Their only chance of making this crazy plan work would be to do it fast, get superlucky, and be insanely bold.

But would they follow him?

Felix, Paul, and Madison nodded their approval of his plan.

Carl and Lee shuffled but stayed with them.

Emma punched Ethan in the shoulder to show her sisterly support.

"Okay," Ethan told them as he rubbed his shoulder (Emma *always* hit him too hard). "Paul and Felix go first, help the others up."

The two boys darted down the hall to the skylight. They hoisted everyone onto the roof.

Ethan helped by pushing people up from beneath . . . and then he was the last one left in Ward Zero. He looked down the hallway, hoping one more kid would come out of their rooms to join them.

No one did.

Ethan understood how it felt to be paralyzed with fear and disbelief. They'd all been raised to respect their parents—every adult. So had he. How could they believe those adults were now the enemy?

He felt sorry for them.

He felt sorry for himself, too, because he knew he'd have nightmares about what the Ch'zar would do to them.

Ethan reached up and took Felix's and Paul's extended hands.

They hauled him up to the roof.

Ethan crouched with them on the clay tiles. No one spoke.

He gestured for them to go to the far corner.

Madison grabbed his arm and gave him a squeeze. She didn't let go.

Ethan peeled her grip off and shook his head.

What was she doing? She couldn't come with him. She had to unlock that gate.

Madison seemed to get it, but she gave Ethan a hurt glare before she moved off.

Girls. Why did they do stuff like that at the worst possible moment? He'd never understand them.

Alone now, he crept to the other corner of the roof and poked his head over the edge.

Adults in athletic suits searched the hospital grounds, spreading out. The building shuddered as a dozen more entered and tromped inside.

Ethan pulled away and looked back. Madison and the others were at the far corner. One by one, they vanished, sliding down the rainspout.

He had to buy them more time.

He swallowed, took a deep breath, checked his footing, and—even though his legs trembled—he stood.

"Hey!" he yelled down at the guards. "I'm right here!"

The adults looked up in unison, their hive mind acting as one.

"I'm Ethan Blackwood from Santa Blanca," he yelled. "I beat you guys before. I'll do it again. Why don't you try to stop me, you—"

With a *thump*, a shoulder-mounted cannon fired—not an artillery shell or laser beam, though. A net *whoosh*ed over Ethan's head. It spread out to a six-by-six foot square, landed next to him, and swished across the roof tiles into a tangling snarl.

If one of those hit him, he could be stuck for minutes. Plenty of time for the adults to get up here and collect him.

He ran for it.

A dozen more cannons thumped.

Nets filled the air where Ethan had stood a second before. More landed behind his feet, to his right, to his left, in front of him.

He leaped over that last net and sprinted to the sky-light.

Ethan skidded to a stop and paused a heartbeat for dramatic effect.

Below, the suited adults tracked him; cannons ratcheted and clicked as they reloaded.

He jumped *over* the skylight and landed flat on the other side.

Ethan hoped from the ground it'd look like he had just dropped *into* the hospital.

He crawled on his stomach to the rainspout.

No adults were on this side . . . yet.

He shimmied down.

Ethan hit the ground and ran to the back of the hospital compound. There were parked garbage trucks near the gate that gave his team decent cover.

Madison cracked the gate's lock and rolled it open.

On the other side was a two-lane road that led into a tunnel. That had to lead out to the other side of Fiesta City.

They'd made it!

Ethan caught up to his friends, and Felix gave him a high five.

Before Ethan could congratulate the rest of them or give his sister a slug on the shoulder, two athletic suits emerged from the tunnel. The teachers inside their cockpits lowered crackling lances at the kids and blocked their only escape.

○ ○ ○ 21 ○ ○ ○

SACRIFICIAL PIECE

ETHAN, FELIX, MADISON, AND PAUL STOOD shoulder to shoulder and raised their fists to fight.

This was crazy. *One* weaponized athletic suit would be more than a match for four kids.

Two would wipe the floor with them.

The Ward Zero kids huddled behind them, clutching one another, terrified. Even Emma.

Ethan didn't blame her.

It was the only *smart* thing to do.

He looked around for a club, a weapon, *anything* to fight with—and found one.

"The gate," Ethan whispered to his friends.

"It's electrified," Felix said, and then his face lit up as he caught on. "Oh . . . it's electrified."

Madison glanced at the sliding gate and then to the two suits lumbering toward them. "I'll do it," she whispered.

Paul turned to the Ward Zero kids. "Stand very still," he warned them.

The two suits lumbered closer, steps shaking the ground, lances crackling, and net cannons swiveling to cover the defending Resisters.

"COME PEACEFULLY," one teacher in a suit boomed over a loudspeaker. "YOU WILL NOT BE HARMED."

"We give up!" Ethan raised his hands. "Just, please, don't hurt us."

He stayed right where he was and let the two suits pound toward him.

The first suit stepped into the gap where the gate had been rolled aside.

Madison leaped forward. She grabbed the electrified gate with gloved hands and slammed it into the athletic suit's steel frame.

A gazillion volts of electricity cracked, buzzed, and shot through the suit. The adult inside the cockpit danced and passed out.

The lights in the hospital and on the fence went dark.

The electrified athletic suit teetered and fell toward them, completely short-circuited and inert.

The second suit, though, pushed through the gate, over its fallen comrade, and charged them.

Ethan was scared out of his mind, but he'd trained for two years in athletic suits on his school's soccer team, the Grizzlies. He knew the suits were powered by hydraulic lines and could lift tons, but those lines were just rubber hoses. They were always failing or popping off. It was the suits' one weakness.

"The hydraulics!" Ethan screamed. "Go for the tubes!"

The teacher shot a net at Paul and Felix.

They dodged and the net fell on the Ward Zero kids, who went down hopelessly tangled.

The teacher thrust his lance at Ethan.

Ethan sidestepped, but it struck so close, the hair on his arms rose toward the electrified steel and he smelled ozone.

Felix, his face a mask of deadly concentration, darted inside the monster's reach and grabbed a fistful of rubber lines, braced with one leg, and pulled with all his might.

The suit swatted him aside.

Felix went flying through the air—clutching three black tubes.

Red hydraulic fluid geysered from the mechanical monster.

It collapsed with a clatter.

Paul moved in, snarling, and kicked the teacher in the cockpit, knocking him out cold.

Ethan couldn't believe it. They'd survived?

Carl, Lee, and Emma untangled themselves from the net. They were shaken but still managed to clap each other on the back and looked as ready to fight as any other Resister.

Madison, Paul, even Felix were okay, although as Felix tried to stand, he couldn't: one of his legs bent at a weird angle.

Ethan's joy faded as he saw blood soak through the thigh of Felix's flight suit.

Everyone was suddenly still and quiet as they saw, too.

"It's broken," Felix told them as calmly as if stating he'd just untied a shoelace.

"We'll splint it," Madison said, and cast about for a length of wood or metal to brace his leg.

Felix met Ethan's eyes and he shook his head.

Ethan understood how bad the situation was. A kid limping around with a bleeding broken leg, even at Sterling, was bound to attract attention. It would slow them all down, too.

But Ethan wouldn't leave Felix behind.

What about the other kids? Emma? Who would get them out if he stayed here?

Ethan shook his head back at Felix.

It didn't matter. He wasn't leaving his friend behind, no matter what. Felix hadn't left *him* behind in Santa Blanca. If he had, Ethan would be part of the Ch'zar right now.

Paul picked up a lance from a fallen athletic suit and handed it to Felix. It was huge but somehow looked right in Felix's hand, as if he were a modern medieval knight.

Another athletic suit tromped around the corner of the hospital. It spotted them. It stood there, and five more suits of armor joined it. They moved together, toward Ethan and the others, spreading out so they couldn't slip back into the hospital.

"I've got this," Felix said. Using the lance as a crutch, he hobbled between the gate and the approaching suits.

"No way!" Ethan and Madison said together.

"Don't you understand?" Paul said, glancing at the athletic suits and back to them. "There's no other choice."

"You've got to get to our suits," Felix said. "You've got to save your sister, Ethan."

Ethan crossed his arms over the chest. He absolutely would not do it.

Madison stood next to him and crossed her arms in the same manner.

Before either could say anything, though, Felix took a deep breath and told them, "I'm still the highest-ranking Resister on this mission. Those are orders."

The six athletic suits had closed half the distance between the hospital and the gate.

Emma looked like she'd follow her brother to the ends of the earth . . . but she also glanced at the incoming suits and grew pale. "Ethan?" she whispered. "What are we going to do?"

Ethan felt like he was dying inside.

Tactically and strategically, Felix was right. But this wasn't like a board game in some class. Felix wasn't a piece to be sacrificed so they could lose the battle but win the war.

All their lives were at stake, though.

Maybe even the continued existence of the Resistance.

Was *that* worth Felix's life?

No.

And . . . yes.

Ethan set a hand on Felix's shoulder. "We'll come back for you, Felix. I promise."

"I know you will," Felix said with a smile.

Something in his honest smile, though, was cold, hard, and sad.

Madison stared at them. "You can't be serious. . . ."

Ethan turned to her, the Ward Zero kids, and Paul. He would have given anything to stay and fight, but he couldn't do that. If he did, the Ch'zar won.

"Move it," he told them, mimicking Felix's got-a-mission-to-do tone. "You heard his orders."

He gave Madison a gentle shove.

She moved, but sluggishly, then seemed to make up her mind, snapped out of it, and helped Lee, Carl, and Emma.

They ran for the tunnel.

Ethan paused and looked back.

Felix raised his lance and roared a battle cry. The mechanical athletic suits closed on him.

More than anything, Ethan wanted to stay and fight, to die if he had to with his friend . . . but instead, he followed Felix's last order: he ran.

○ ○ ○ 22 ○ ○ ○

THE STERLING SCHOOL RIOT

ETHAN MARCHED DOWN THE WALKWAYS OF the Sterling campus. It was a beautiful afternoon. Birds twittered and the air smelled of fresh-cut grass.

He felt like a rotten coward and a quitter for leaving Felix to fight a hopeless battle.

But what choice did he have?

Ethan suddenly got why Colonel Winter was so mean all the time. He bet she had to make these life-and-death, every-option-was-bad type of choices all the time.

Felix wouldn't last long against those athletic suits.

Especially with a broken leg. He'd go down fighting, though, until they netted and stunned him.

And then . . . ?

The Ch'zar wouldn't kill him. They'd interrogate Felix. He'd resist. And then they'd—

Madison jabbed him in the ribs.

"We need your brain on this mission." Her gaze fixed straight ahead, but Ethan saw tears gleaming in her eyes. "We have to get back to our suits."

"Right," Ethan said.

That would be the only way they'd get out alive. That was their *only* chance to rescue Felix.

So he kept moving.

Ethan inhaled, getting a whiff of everyone in his group. They stank.

They'd just come from Sterling's laundry. They'd gotten Carl, Lee, and Emma sets of smelly black sweats like everyone else. Ethan had found a set of teachers' sweats, though, and changed into those. It was the same basic black but had a silver *S* embroidered over the heart. That might come in handy.

They moved quickly and quietly as Paul led them toward the front gate. They kept to the shadows. Classes would still be in session. There were only a few kids outside now, obviously cutting class.

The plan was to blend with the kids after the last class and slip into Fiesta City.

His mind flashed back to Felix, standing there with that stupid lance, about to get squished by six robotic opponents.

He *couldn't* think of him. He had to keep sharp, focused.

Ethan glanced at his sister. He needed her strength. They'd always gotten into—and out of—trouble together.

Her brown eyes met his.

She'd changed. She looked as if she'd aged a few years in the last few weeks. The easy smile that had always seemed to be on her lips was gone, replaced with lines of worry. Who wouldn't be changed after all she'd been through? He wondered what he looked like to her now.

Emma's eyes focused past Ethan . . . and widened with terror.

He followed her gaze.

Two walkways over, an athletic suit marched parallel alongside them.

Ethan turned to Madison to warn her but saw three *more* suits marching with them one sidewalk away on the other side, mirroring their progress.

That was no coincidence.

Ethan had to do something. They needed a distraction so they could get away from those mechanical monsters.

On the brick wall ahead was a fire alarm. He walked faster, straight for it.

"Don't!" Paul whispered.

Ethan wrenched the alarm's lever down.

Cameras on the walls nearby flashed, capturing Ethan's profile on two sides.

Ethan blinked, recovering his sight, and then figured out what'd just happened.

Of course. Sterling would have a way to see whoever triggered the alarm. In a school full of delinquent kids, it'd be too tempting a target otherwise.

Class bells rang in short, shrill bursts.

Kids poured out of the classrooms, grinning and whooping it up, happy to be released early. Not one of them took the fire alarm seriously.

Over the campus loudspeakers, a voice boomed, "ALL STUDENTS WALK TO THEIR DESIGNATED EMERGENCY ASSEMBLY AREAS."

The Sterling kids ignored this, so teachers came out and herded them along.

Ethan and his crew got pushed along in the tide of jostling students.

Paul shoved his way to Ethan and then gave Ethan a

shove for good measure. "Great," he muttered. "Those cameras feed into the front office. Every teacher just got a look at *your* face. They know where we are!"

Ethan spied teachers from every direction now moving toward them, *against* the flow of students. Athletic suits tromped onto the covered sidewalks, too. They slammed aside any students who happened to be in their way.

This was it.

The Ch'zar had them. They were trapped. It was his fault, too.

Ethan felt like he was in a whirlpool, getting pulled deeper, about to drown.

One kid in the crowd waved at him.

He should have ignored her, thought of a scheme to get them out of this, or heroically sacrificed himself for the others like Felix had done, but it was that *crazy* girl, the one in the gang who'd almost beat them up in Fiesta City, and the same one who'd then rescued him on the P.E. field.

She flicked her fingers through her short hair, popped bubble gum, and grinned at him.

If *anyone* deserved to be in a mental hospital like Ward Zero, it was her.

She was nuts. She'd fight *anything, anywhere.*

Which gave Ethan just the idea he needed.

He jumped onto a railing between the sidewalk and the lawn. He literally stood out from the crowd. No teacher or student could miss him.

"Listen up!" Ethan shouted. "This is an extra credit exercise for P.E.! FIGHT—teachers versus students!"

Every Sterling kid turned to him and their mouths dropped open.

The teachers froze in their tracks as the Ch'zar hive mind tried to figure this out.

No one for sure knew what to make of him. He wore teachers' sweats but could no way pass for an adult.

"READY . . . SET . . . GO!" Ethan screamed.

For a heartbeat, no one moved.

Then the crazy, gum-chewing girl warbled a war cry. She grabbed a clump of sod from the lawn and side-armed it right into the face of a teacher!

The teacher went down, sputtering and scraping mud from his eyes.

Everyone shouted and started chucking dirt clods and books. Students screamed and tackled teachers. A dozen clung on to one athletic suit and toppled it.

It was complete hysteria.

Ethan had started a riot!

A rock *spang*ed off the wall near his head. He ducked and shoved his way back to his crew. They stood back-to-back and kicked and punched anyone who came hear them.

"The gate," Ethan mouthed at Paul over the noise.

Paul flashed him a glare like he'd just done the most stupid thing in the universe, but nodded and ran down the covered sidewalk.

Ethan moved after him, Madison alongside him as wingman, and they cleared a path for Lee, Carl, and Emma.

He kept a careful eye on those athletic suits.

They were everywhere—on the sidewalks, lawns, and a few on the rooftops as spotters—but none came for them. They couldn't. The entire school had become one mass battle of wild, yelling students.

The Sterling kids grabbed, punched, and pulled the hair of every teacher who had bossed them around. They even attacked more of the athletic suits. Kids jumped onto their frames, took the lances out of their hands, and started using the weapons against them!

Ethan and his crew stayed close to the walls and kept moving forward.

Shadows flashed overhead—shapes that zoomed above the cloud cover.

Ch'zar I.C.E. suits. Firefly reconnaissance. Maybe a Thunderbolt-class locust.

Would the Ch'zar use brute force to stop this? The Sterling kids would see the I.C.E. armor and freak out for sure. They'd panic and scatter . . . or maybe even start an all-out war.

Ethan had to get out *now*.

The path ahead was clear. They sprinted for the gate.

That was when Ethan noticed they'd picked up three more in their group.

One, of course, was the crazy girl who chewed gum, another was the dark-skinned boy who Ethan had bested in tactics class, and the third was the bruiser from the same class who could have given Felix a match in a wrestling contest.

Ethan let them straggle along. He'd take *any* help he could get at this point—even from that not-so-mentally-stable girl.

Ethan got to the front gate and climbed over.

His crew followed, as did more Sterling kids.

It seemed like half the school climbed over the gates and walls and spilled into Fiesta City. The troublemakers broke windows, set fires, and got chased by more teachers tromping after them in athletic suits.

Ethan ran past arcades, pizza parlors, through the carnival midway, and eventually tumbled down the bank of the dry riverbed on the outskirts of town. He took cover in the lengthening afternoon shadows.

Overhead insect wings thrummed, pausing and circling, but then headed into the city.

Ethan exhaled.

Next to him, Madison panted, as did Paul. Carl and Lee looked green, but also relieved to be far from Sterling. Emma's face was lined with concern as she kept looking around, listening, and waiting for the Ch'zar to land and take them back.

The three "normal" Sterling kids, though, looked expectantly at Ethan.

The gum-chewing girl sidled up to him and took his arm. "So, what now?" she asked. "Blow up the dormitories?"

Emma pulled the girl away. "Don't get near my brother," she said.

Madison looked like she was about to back Emma up, quite possibly with a roundhouse kick to the Sterling girl's head!

"It's okay," Ethan said, raising his hands between the girls.

They couldn't afford a fight here.

"I'm Kristov," the big Sterling kid told him. His nose

was flattened, broken and set that way. "The brainy guy is Oliver, and the girl with the bad haircut who can't keep her mouth shut is Angel. You're trying to escape. Can we come?"

He held out a huge hand for Ethan to shake.

Ethan took it, wondering if he'd regret it later.

"We're not *trying* to escape," Ethan said. "We *are* escaping. You're welcome to come—but you may not like what you're getting into."

Ethan led them down the dry riverbed, sticking to the shadows. "I'm going to tell you a story," he said, "a crazy, impossible story about Earth, an invasion, why you're here, and why we came to break you out. Then I'm going to prove it's all true."

He led them into the cave where they'd stashed their I.C.E. suits.

° ° ° 23 ° ° °

BUILT TO DESTROY

ETHAN BUZZED OVER FIESTA CITY AT TWO
hundred miles an hour. It was dusk and the carnival lights
flashed on with a million colors.

His wasp painted laser fire over the top of the roller
coaster where Ch'zar recon firefly units perched, camou-
flaged among the glowing strobe lights.

The tiny bugs burst into flames.

Paul's praying mantis slammed into the red-hot tracks.
He tipped the structure over onto two Thunderbolt-class
locusts on the ground with a tremendous *SCREEECH*,
squishing them flat.

"Hurry up," Madison piped over the radio. She circled overhead in her dragonfly. "That stirred up the nest. Two dozen units inbound to our position. Locusts. Fast-intercept wasps, too."

"Good," Ethan replied. "Stick to the plan. We'll meet you at the rendezvous point."

"Roger that," Paul replied, sounding doubtful.

"Good luck," Madison said. She hesitated like she wanted to tell him more, but then just added, "Over and out."

The plan. One in a series of desperate schemes today. How long would Ethan's luck hold? The plan was this: they'd make trouble in Fiesta City and get the Ch'zar to chase Paul and Madison as they fled.

That was the *easy* part.

Ethan's job was to then sneak in and rescue Felix . . . where a million things could go wrong.

First, he had to wrestle with his wasp's mind, cool the insect's instinct to go on a killing spree and destroy everything in Fiesta City.

He tapped the dark purple controls and put his wasp into stealth mode.

Ethan flew low, in the shadows, his wings whisper quiet.

None of the firefly recon units overhead followed.

So far, so good.

Not so good was what had happened fifteen minutes before.

Ethan had told Kristov, Oliver, and Angel the story of the Ch'zar invading Earth. He explained how they used a form of mind control that only worked on the adults and how they raised kids in perfect neighborhoods . . . until they grew up and got added to the collective alien intelligence.

Carl, Lee, and Emma had already seen enough to piece together the truth. That's why they'd been stuck in Ward Zero.

The three normal Sterling kids had *no* clue, though, and didn't believe Ethan.

Until they were face to face with the Resistance's I.C.E. suits.

Then all six kids freaked out. Who wouldn't?

Ethan had almost fainted the first time he'd seen the giant insects.

Carl and Oliver had run at the sight of them, although Madison had stopped them before they got too far. Emma had been transfixed with terror.

But Ethan then showed them that the I.C.E. suits were tame, really half machine, and he opened his wasp's cockpit to show them the interior.

After a few minutes, Madison had had to peel Angel away from her dragonfly.

Ethan promised them they'd get the training to fly suits like these, but first he had to rescue Felix.

The Resisters didn't leave their people behind.

They ushered the Sterling kids into the assault carrier moth and set its autopilot to move away when it got dark.

Madison and Paul would shake their pursuers and catch up to provide an escort.

He hoped.

Emma and the others in that moth depended on everything about his plan going right.

Ethan let out a long sigh.

They *all* depended on him and his plans. What if he was wrong?

He directed his wasp to land on the Sterling chemistry lab's roof. The insect's gold-and-black stripes were good camouflage in the fading shadows.

He waited and watched the last glow of the sunset fade.

The campus below was deserted. The Sterling students had moved into Fiesta City. Fires burned there.

Ethan felt sorry for the kids. They'd lose this battle. The Ch'zar would send as many adults or I.C.E. units to capture them as they needed. And then what? Would the

Ch'zar put them back in school after this? Would they chemically trigger puberty and force them into the hive mind?

Ethan wished he could save them all.

One day everyone would be free of the Ch'zar. Right now, though, he had to make some hard choices. The first being how to infiltrate and assault Ward Zero and get Felix out alive.

He jumped off the roof and silently buzzed over to the hospital. The complex was ringed with a dozen teachers in athletic suits.

But no I.C.E. units. That was a lucky break.

Ethan attacked.

He landed on one suit, crunching its steel frame, pinning the teacher inside. Two more athletic suits whirled and raised their lances.

The wasp was faster.

It lashed out with its forelimbs, ripping mechanical arms and legs off, leaving the teachers inside stunned, their suits spurting hydraulic fluid.

A half-dozen more sprinted toward Ethan.

Laser fire took them out at the knees before they crossed half the distance.

He had to find Felix before I.C.E. reinforcements arrived.

Thanks to the Ch'zar telepathic hive mind, they all knew he was here.

He reached for the cockpit release. Ethan would search this hospital room by room to find Felix. Assuming Felix was even here.

Ethan felt the wasp's impatience at his indecision. The insect wanted to fight, to rip things apart and kill. Inside his wasp's mind were images of them attacking an enemy wasp's nest—tearing, ripping, biting the larva inside, eating things.

Ethan mentally backed off. It was supergross.

But not entirely a bad idea.

Not the eating part, though. Ick. He'd forgotten that his wasp was built to destroy rival insect nests. And with that superdense molecular surface that Dr. Irving had told him about, concrete and brick were as weak as tissue paper to the wasp.

He leaped to the hospital's roof.

The wasp grasped tiles with its barbed forelimbs and raked up. Wooden beams and drywall and air ducts tore away.

Underneath were the student rooms, all empty, so Ethan pulled up more roof, using the wasp's wings to boost his lifting power. He ripped away an entire corner, crashed through room after room, cinder blocks crumbling like Styrofoam under the wasp's incredible strength.

Ethan demolished the second floor, and he started on the ground level, tearing the concrete walls apart.

He found the kitchen, the generator room, more student dormitories, and a few adults, who scattered before the wasp.

Finally he got to a room with white-tiled walls where Felix lay strapped to a gurney.

Felix struggled against his bonds. Adults stood around him. They held syringes and one even had a scalpel in hand.

What were they doing to him?

The wasp's anger flooded Ethan's brain.

He fought it, gaining control to hold back at the last moment before the wasp could pick up the adults and squish them. Instead, the insect merely swatted them aside.

He could've killed them all. It would've been easy.

But what good was that?

The adults weren't to blame. It was the Ch'zar. Even if he had destroyed every adult here, the aliens would have a hundred thousand more to take their place.

The wasp towered over Felix.

With one precisely controlled slash, he severed the straps holding his friend.

Sweat covered Felix's face and he trembled.

They'd probably tried to make him talk and done terrible things to him.

Ethan's heart twisted and tightened.

"Took you long enough," Felix whispered. His eyelids fluttered as he struggled through the pain to stay awake.

Ethan popped the cockpit hatch and climbed out to help his friend.

"Sorry I'm late," Ethan replied. "Looks like you were taking it easy anyway."

Felix chuckled and winced. "You got out? All of you?"

"Yeah, more than we started with, even," Ethan whispered. "Can you fly? I have your beetle close. The moth carried it, just a quick jump outside the city."

Felix let out a long exhale and his eyes eased shut.

Ethan noticed that bruises covered Felix's body. His leg hadn't been set. Beads of sweat covered his face.

Ethan panicked and shook Felix. "Stay with me. Don't . . ."

He couldn't say, *"Don't die."*

If Felix died, Ethan didn't know what he'd do.

Go crazy? Let his wasp rampage and kill everything? Sit here, cry, and give up?

Felix's eyes fluttered open. With a gasp and a grunt, he grabbed Ethan's hand and pulled himself up. "Guess I can't lie around here slacking any longer," he whispered.

Ethan took Felix's arm, looped it around his neck, and helped him sit.

He glanced up at the star-filled sky through the ruined hospital, blinking away the tears that had started to prick his eyes. There was no way he could let Felix see him cry.

"We have to move fast," he told Felix. "When Ch'zar reinforcements come, we can't get caught in the open."

"I can move," Felix told him, grimacing in pain. "And fight, if I have to. That's not what I'm worried about." He looked Ethan square in the eye.

A chill shuddered through Ethan.

He knew what Felix meant.

Sure, they'd fought Ch'zar patrols, infiltrated Fiesta City and the Sterling School, rescued a half-dozen kids— even Ethan's sister—and outsmarted the enemy at every turn so far.

But now they had to go back to the Seed Bank and face the greatest danger of this mission: Felix's mother, Colonel Winter.

○ ○ ○ **24** ○ ○ ○

MASSIVE SEARCH AND DESTROY

ETHAN TOOK POINT AS THEY APPROACHED
the Seed Bank, even ahead of Madison's scouting dragonfly.

He'd insisted.

It didn't matter who had the highest rank anymore.
Ethan led this group. It'd been his crazy idea to go. He
was responsible for them all. If the Seed Bank decided to
shoot them out of the air for desertion, disobeying orders,
and treason, he was going to be the one they blasted first.

Madison's sleek green blur of a dragonfly was behind
him, somehow looking annoyed that it had to fly so slowly.
Felix trailed her, his enormous rhinoceros beetle steady

despite its pilot being crippled. Paul's praying mantis looped around the luna moth carrier. The mantis's head darted back and forth, searching for enemies to tear apart.

The screens in Ethan's cockpit went dead.

On his center screen flashed:

SECURITY PROTOCOL 003

Ethan fidgeted in the suddenly dark and claustrophobic cockpit. There were no radio transmissions allowed during the mandatory blackout period.

He was alone with his worries.

How many seconds would he have in which to explain everything before Colonel Winter had him arrested? Or shot? Would he even have time to tell her that his plan had worked?

The cockpit's cameras snapped back on.

Blue landing lights spiraled through the tunnel head, guiding his wasp into the heart of the mountain where the Seed Bank nestled.

Deeper and deeper the wasp descended until the ultraviolet-tinged glow of the hangar's lights flashed ahead. Poised at the tunnel mouth, two machine guns pointed into the tunnel. They were the big fifty-millimeters that fired depleted uranium rounds. The Resisters mounted them on the Behemoth-class centipede crawlers to take out Ch'zar ant lions.

What were those guns doing here?

They tracked the wasp . . . but held their fire.

Ethan, his heart practically stopped, passed over them and landed.

The wasp fluttered its wings once and settled down.

Those guns were new. Had the Resisters installed the heavy weapons because of *them*?

The other I.C.E. suits in his group landed in a line next to his wasp. The luna moth carrier touched down as light as a feather but still sent shudders through the metal deck from its incredible weight.

Standing alongside him might be the last thing Madison, Felix, and Paul would do as Resister pilots. Ethan was proud to call them his friends (well, maybe that feeling didn't apply to Paul).

Ethan expected a bunch of guards to be there, ready to take them away at gunpoint.

But that wasn't happening. Yet.

In the hangar were technicians, officers, a dozen other pilots, and, yeah, even a few guards with sidearms, but they were prepping I.C.E. suits, moving supplies and ammunition, filling out paperwork, all 100 percent serious.

Hardly *anyone* noticed them.

A set of elevator doors parted.

Colonel Winter, Dr. Irving, and three adult officers stepped off. Colonel Winter pointed at Ethan's group and strode toward them.

Ethan quickly went through his shutdown checklist. He engaged the safeties on the wasp's laser and put the insect brain into hibernation mode. He wasn't about to let some tech get flattened or burned to a crisp because he was a sloppy pilot.

He punched the cockpit release and climbed out.

Ethan patted his wasp for the last time, took a deep breath, and went to meet his fate.

Madison helped Felix struggle out of his beetle's cockpit. He gritted his teeth from the pain of his broken leg and other injuries. Paul looked at them and then at Ethan. His expression flickered from anger, to resolve, and then finally to something close to admiration—not like they were friends or anything, but at least maybe they weren't mortal enemies anymore.

Technicians approached their I.C.E. suits and attached biomonitors. One tech pulled the flight recorders and disappeared into the elevator.

"The starboard wing," Ethan told one tech (*starboard* referred to the right-hand side of a ship or plane). "The leading edge took a hit."

The technician scowled at the hasty caterpillar patch job and nodded.

Ethan then joined his crew to face Colonel Winter.

But she, Dr. Irving, and her senior staff had stopped at the luna moth carrier, helping the kids from Sterling clamber out. She directed doctors to check them, covered them in blankets, and helped hand out self-heating field rations and cartons of milk.

Dr. Irving caught Ethan's confused gaze, cocked a bushy white eyebrow, and waved him over.

"Let's get this over with," Ethan whispered. He looped Felix's arm around his shoulder and they hobbled forward.

Officers stood aside for them; some glared while a few raised their eyebrows. The Resister pilots their age stopped their duties and looked at Ethan, stunned and awed that they had the bravado to approach the colonel.

Who would willingly march up to get court-martialed?

Only complete idiots.

"I'm relieved you made it back safe," Colonel Winter said to the gathered Sterling kids. She spoke in the warmest tone Ethan had ever heard from her. That had to be a trick of some sort.

"I'm sure you were briefed on our situation, recent history, and our mission," the colonel continued. "You undoubtedly have *more* questions. We will answer them, but first we must make certain you're unharmed. Please be patient and go with Dr. Irving."

The Sterling kids gawked with wonder and terror at the hundreds of I.C.E. suits, the soldiers with guns, and then glanced back at Ethan.

Emma smiled at him.

She must have sensed something was wrong, because it was an uneasy, "Are we *really* safe?" smile.

He smiled back at her and the rest of them as best he could.

He wasn't sure what was going to happen next, but he couldn't let *them* know that.

Dr. Irving came up to Emma. "This is your sister, Ethan?"

"Yes, sir," Ethan replied. "Emma, this is Dr. Gordon Irving. He's a . . . friend."

Was he?

He stared into the doctor's eyes.

He liked the old man. He was Madison's grandfather. Maybe the founder of the Seed Bank. But he worked with Colonel Winter, who seemed happy to throw kids into her brig until they grew up. Could he trust the doctor with his sister and the other kids he'd risked everything to save?

Dr. Irving gave Ethan the tiniest nod. If Ethan had blinked, he'd have missed it.

Something was going on here beyond him and his team rescuing the Sterling kids.

"I'll catch up to you soon," Ethan told Emma. "I promise."

Emma still looked worried, but she relaxed a notch.

He told all the kids, "It's okay. We made it. You're safe."

At least they were safe in one way: No matter what the colonel did to them, their minds would still be their own—not controlled by the Ch'zar Collective and sealed inside an enemy I.C.E. suit. That was the most important thing.

Emma, Carl, and Lee followed Dr. Irving and Colonel Winter's senior staff to the elevators.

The Sterling School troublemakers, though, Angel, Kristov, and Oliver, lingered.

They glared at Colonel Winter. Maybe they'd never trust an authority figure like her, or maybe they sensed that Ethan was up to his neck in hot water and needed help. They looked ready to fight . . . if he gave them the word.

Ethan wouldn't let them get dragged into his troubles.

"We're good here," he told them.

Angel sighed and swallowed her gum, seeming disappointed there wasn't going to be another fight, but she suddenly looked exhausted, too.

She and her friends reluctantly went to Dr. Irving as he held the elevator for them.

Colonel Winter then focused her full attention on Ethan and his crew with a hawklike gaze. She tapped the tablet computer in her hand twice and said, "Good work, you four."

Ethan felt as if she'd slapped him in the face with a steel gauntlet.

He blinked and croaked out a whispered, "Pardon me, ma'am?"

She ignored him and glanced at Felix's bent leg. "Broken?"

"Yes, Colonel," Felix said, managing to stand straighter and look tough. "Just a simple fracture. Nothing serious this time."

The colonel touched his cheek. It was the same gesture Ethan's mom would have done if he'd skinned his knee. It was a touch only a loving mother could give her child.

She stepped back and she was Colonel Winter again, Felix's commanding officer.

"We'll get you patched up in no time." She turned her tablet computer around so they could see the screen. "Which is fortunate because there's still work to be done."

Ethan *still* wasn't understanding. Was this a dream?

He squinted at the colonel's tablet, expecting it to be

the official order for their courts-martial and summary executions.

It wasn't.

On-screen was a map. There were the same enemy bug icons that he and Madison had seen on Dr. Irving's computer. There were dozens of them, each standing for hundreds of individual Ch'zar units. Arrows showed direction of movement and speed. They crisscrossed over the eastern side of the United States—Alabama, Kentucky, all the way up to Maine, and over the entire Appalachian Mountains.

Like he had with the board game in Sterling's Tactics 101 class, Ethan instantly got the rules and implications of this map.

It was a superlarge-scale search-and-destroy mission.

That wouldn't have been possible before, but now the enemy had the vast numbers to carry out such a brute-force operation.

"The Ch'zar search every square inch of the mountain range," the colonel told them. "They're uprooting trees, turning over boulders, and placing seismic sensors. They are coming for us. They will find the Seed Bank unless we stop them. It is only a matter of time. Ten days at most."

This was a disaster.

But Ethan still didn't understand why they weren't all in the brig for going AWOL and disobeying her direct order about going to Sterling.

He just had to know.

He gathered all his courage and asked, "And this is why we're not in trouble?"

"Trouble, Mr. Blackwood?" Colonel Winter's eyebrows shot up in mock surprise. "Indeed, we are *all* in trouble." She glanced about the hangar to see if anyone was within earshot. "Or perhaps you mean this last mission? When I called for volunteers to go on a high-risk rescue operation to recruit suitable pilot candidates to repel this force? You recovered six trainees—an entire squadron willing to accept the truth and fight the Ch'zar. It was much more than I had hoped for. Congratulations."

Ethan's mouth dropped open.

Fortunately, Madison was a quicker thinker than Ethan. She kicked his foot. "Yes, ma'am," she said. "That's *exactly* what Blackwood meant."

"Very good," Colonel Winter growled, and tilted her chin up so it felt like she looked down on them all. "Because if that were *not* the case, if this had *not* been a top-secret but *authorized* mission, we would be short our best four pilots precisely when we needed them the most."

Ethan glanced at Madison, Felix, and Paul.

They all looked as stunned as he felt, but they all had the sense to keep their mouths shut.

"Sergeant, get that leg tended to," Colonel Winter told Felix. She slapped her tablet. "Our projections of Ch'zar movement give us one week to get those Sterling kids ready."

"Ready for what?" Ethan asked.

"You four will lead them through a comprehensive emergency course on piloting I.C.E. suits. And I hope it is not a crash course," Colonel Winter said, "because our lives may depend on them."

∘ ∘ ∘ 25 ∘ ∘ ∘

ALMOST IDENTICAL

ETHAN STOOD ON THE CATWALK THAT overlooked the Seed Bank farming cavern.

A hundred feet below were fields of wheat and corn, artificial rivers that meandered, and herds of zebra that grazed. Overhead, a constellation of artificial sun globes cast enough light for a midsummer day.

Ethan could almost believe he was outside (maybe it was built this way so people down here didn't get completely claustrophobic). Only a whiff of recirculated air and the curve of the great walls gave away that you weren't outside.

Ethan hesitated on the catwalk, standing outside a steel door. This was the same room they'd stuck him in when he'd first come to the Seed Bank.

There were hundreds of these tiny rooms up here, although officers, regular pilots, and just about everyone else lived in larger quarters on another level.

So who had these rooms been built for? Had there been thousands of Resisters in the past? Or had these been for people who never made it to the Seed Bank before the Ch'zar invasion?

He'd ask Dr. Irving, but not now.

Ethan was here for Emma.

He knocked.

There was silence, and then Emma called from inside. "Come in?"

Ethan opened the door.

His sister sat on a cot, her legs drawn up to her chest. There were tearstains on her freckled cheeks. Her long braid wrapped around her neck. She had on jeans and a pink T-shirt the Resisters must have given her.

She perked up at the sight of Ethan, jumped to her feet, and hugged him.

"Thank you!" she murmured. "Thank you *so* much."

He awkwardly hugged her back.

He didn't know what to say. She didn't have to *thank*

him for anything. He only wished he'd figured out earlier that the Ch'zar had taken her to Sterling. He should've guessed that.

She pushed him away, slugged him in the shoulder, and sat back on the cot.

"It's been one long nightmare," she said, squeezing the last tears from her eyes, and then stared off into space. "And it's not over yet, is it?"

Ethan shook his head. "Not until the Ch'zar are destroyed."

Emma snorted. "A month ago, all I could think about were finals and getting into Vassar Prep. I was worried about the Senior Elementary Prom, for crying out loud! I had the dress picked out, the corsage, even got the boy to—" She smacked her fist into her hand so hard, Ethan flinched from his sister's uncharacteristic violence. "I was *so* deluded."

"I know how you feel," Ethan whispered.

He, too, had bought the lie of a life that had been his Santa Blanca neighborhood. It'd been so nice he almost wished he could go back there . . . if not for that whole "lose your mind when you became an adult" thing.

"I've got to forget that stuff now," Emma said, her mouth tightening into a grim frown. "I *kind of* understand what's going on, from what I've seen and heard from you,

and from what some of the people here have told me."
Her eyes focused to that laser-intense gaze she had when
she studied trigonometry or Latin. "So let me see if I've
got it straight: these Ch'zar aliens invaded the world and
zapped everyone with mind control?"

"Mind control that only works on adults," Ethan said.
"They get absorbed into one hive mind."

"And that's why the Ch'zar built our neighborhood?"
she asked. "So all the kids will grow up nice and easy?
Then be mind-controlled?"

"Santa Blanca and hundreds of neighborhoods like it."

"That night when the school burned down," Emma
continued, "you were *inside* one of those insects—just like
we were flying back in that luna moth, right? How does
it work?"

"I.C.E. armor," Ethan explained. "I.C.E. stands for
'Insectoid Combat Exoskeleton.' The Resisters use the
Ch'zar's own technology against them. They're part
mechanical and part living insect."

Emma's face curled with revulsion.

"It's not so gross," he said. "And there's a connection
you make to the bug's brain so you can completely control it."

Ethan left out the part how the connection was *two-*

way and it gave pilots a glimpse into the savage, killer insect mind.

Emma would find that out soon enough.

She shuddered out a sigh and changed the subject. "I miss Mom and Dad. Even the twins."

Ethan sat next to her on the cot.

The last time he'd seen his parents was when Coach Norman had taken him away.

As if Emma had read his thoughts, she said, "The day you vanished, when Coach Norman took you, that's when everything turned upside down. The school board moved up the time for my early admission. Mom and Dad acted so kind . . . and so sad. I thought they were just going to miss me since I'd be at Vassar Prep."

Emma wiped her nose, paused midswipe, and turned to him, suddenly looking half panicked. "Mom and Dad left me a goodbye note in my purse. I found it at Sterling. I kept it hidden. I don't know . . . it felt like this huge secret that I couldn't even tell the other kids. I think it *proves* they're not part of this hive mind thing you're talking about."

Ethan's eyes widened. Their parents had left her a note, too?

He'd started to believe that his parents possibly being normal, not being part of the Ch'zar Collective, might've been just his imagination. Unless he was on a mission, he always carried their note. He'd take it out every day and read it to prove to himself it was real, to prove there was hope he'd see his mom and dad again one day.

"Let me see it," he said.

Emma dug a worn envelope from her jean's pocket and set her note on the cot.

Ethan got out his. "They left me one, too."

They traded.

Ethan read his sister's:

3lst May

Emma,

We wish we could explain. You can't come back to save us, though. You might suspect part of the truth.

If you do, you will know why we cannot explain.

We will be safe.

Ethan is likely already gone. There's nothing any of us can do for him now.

The priority is to save yourself. You're more important to humanity than you can know.

Be safe, darling. Keep your head.
It is our wish that someday there will
be zero trouble and the four of us will be
reunited under the open sky; then the two of us
will explain everything.

Two big hugs,
Mom and Dad

They traded back their notes.

"They're *almost* identical," she whispered. "Weird . . . But it has to mean Mom and Dad *are* different from the other Ch'zar-controlled adults, doesn't it?" Hope shone in her eyes.

"I've been thinking about that a lot," Ethan said, wanting to hope, too, but knowing how impossible it seemed. "It could be a Ch'zar trick."

"But it *is* possible," Emma countered, "for some part of the human population to be immune to their mind control?"

Ethan shrugged. "What are the odds of *two* people like that being our mom and dad? That's an awfully big coincidence."

Emma drew her knees back up to her chest and hugged them. "Maybe we'll never know."

They sat a moment in silence.

A sickening wave of homesickness washed through Ethan.

He took a deep breath and stood.

"I don't want to talk about Mom and Dad anymore. It hurts too much, and there's more important things to do." He moved toward the door.

Emma bonked her head onto her knees. "I feel like I'm going to barf."

"I know," Ethan said. "I threw up every day when I first got here. But we've got to beat the Ch'zar. After, then we can figure out what happened to Mom and Dad. I came to show you how we're going to fight them."

She looked up and new determination sparkled in her eyes. "Fight? I can fight," she said. "Those bugs owe me a set of parents, a life, and a senior elementary prom!"

Ethan smiled at her. He knew she was scared, but she was joking and putting on a brave face. "Come on, then," he said, getting up and making for the door.

Emma pulled herself up and followed him down spirals of stairs, through the power generation core, and to the elevator that took them to the repair-and-refit hangar.

As they entered the cavernous room, she moved closer to Ethan.

Surrounding them were hundreds of I.C.E. suits.

Many were being fixed and reloaded with fresh power packs, ammunition, and food cells. Most, though, were in deep hibernation mode, because the Resisters had many more suits than pilots to fly them.

There were gigantic ten-ton Goliath beetles that could barely get airborne, delicate lacewing scouts, Hydra-class millipede assault units, wasps of red and black and gold and green, and even smaller versions of the silver ant lions Ethan had faced before in battle.

Madison sat by her dragonfly as a technician welded a puncture. She watched his every move, providing helpful (and possibly annoying) suggestions.

Ethan waved her over to them.

"We're going to train you and the other Sterling kids to fly," Ethan told Emma.

"Me?" Emma made a gag face. "*Inside* one of these things?"

He ignored her reaction. "There'll only be time to train with one unit," he said.

Ethan left out *why* there'd be so little time: that they'd all be going into battle in a few days.

Madison jogged up to them and flashed Emma one of her crooked smiles.

Ethan had a feeling those two could become good friends.

Emma, though, was too horrified with the zoo of insects around her to make small talk with Madison.

His sister's face then brightened as her gaze landed on one particular I.C.E. suit. "How about that? It's . . . uh, cute."

Ethan had never heard anyone use that word to describe *any* I.C.E. armor. *Powerful*, yes. *Unstoppable*, for sure. But never *cute*.

Madison clapped her hands. "Oh, good choice!"

She and Emma trotted to a half-spherical shape in the shadows. Its shell was covered in dust but still gleamed candy-apple red nonetheless in the dim light.

It was a four-ton ladybug.

"*Coccinella septempunctata*, the seven-spotted lady-bug," Madison explained. "It's the same species Colonel Winter flew when she was a pilot. It's an assault-scout hybrid. Fairly fast, although still subsonic, with twin class-E particle cannons and multiple individually targeting missile pods. Formidable."

"And cute," Emma breathed.

She reached out to touch it, hesitated, but finally found the courage to run a finger over its glass-smooth shell.

She turned to Ethan, grinning. "So, when can I fly him?"

∘ ∘ ∘ 26 ∘ ∘ ∘

TOTAL WASHOUT

ETHAN'S LASER BLASTED THREE MOSQUI-
toes as they hovered in a tight ball of a formation. His
wasp overran their position, scattering the rest as he rocketed to where he'd last seen Emma's ladybug.

The air was a tangle of missile vapor trails, blurred
locust wings, and spirals of red sparks left from Emma's
class-E particle beam.

His sister was nowhere to be seen.

"Emma, report!" he cried over the radio.

There was an explosion ahead—a puffball of flames
and spinning shrapnel and insect limbs.

Emma's ladybug emerged without a scratch on its glistening red armor.

"I'm okay, little brother," she shouted back over the radio.

Her ladybug waggled its antennae his way.

The four-ton beetle was compact and too smooth for an enemy to easily grab. That thing could get deep behind enemy formations and *kill* its way out.

Ethan had to fix his thinking, though, because it wasn't *just* the bug. It was Emma, his sister—the careful, studious, prissy one, the girl who'd a month ago only worried about grades and the prom and boys—piloting as if she were born to it.

She was good. Really good.

Madison called her the best natural pilot she'd ever seen.

Better than him?

That shouldn't matter. Ethan wasn't jealous . . . just concerned (and annoyed) that his sister might be getting in over her head.

Especially since they were in the middle of an *ambush*!

Okay, sure, this was today's *simulated* flight practice after their aerodynamics lecture, but the new recruits still should have been taking it seriously.

Everyone was burned out, though. It'd been a grueling week of nonstop drills, physical training, and homework.

The Sterling kids got five hours of sleep a night before they crawled back into their I.C.E. suits and repeated the process the next day. They were exhausted and getting on each other's nerves.

That went *double* for their instructors.

Ethan, Madison, Felix, and Paul had run out of patience with the new trainees about three days ago.

"Watch out!" Madison screamed over the radio.

Laser fire crisscrossed the smoke-filled air in front of Ethan's wasp.

Stupid. Daydreaming in the middle of a battle drill.

Buzzing mosquitoes filled his cockpit's screens.

It was the half-dozen remaining Thunderbolt-class locusts out there, though, that were the real threat. They were strong enough to tear any one of their I.C.E. suits apart.

Three of the giant grasshopper-like terrors flew straight at Angel.

She'd picked an all-black wasp, Nightmare-class, to train in. The black wasp had superior stealth systems and maneuverability, but lighter armor than Ethan's standard Infiltrator wasp.

Ethan imagined the airspace in his head. It was complicated. Any unit could move up, down, right, left, or diagonal. It was nothing like the game in Sterling's Tactics 101 class. A few key ideas, though, still applied. Like the Resister pilots were too far apart to support one another.

Ethan opened a channel to Felix. "We have to regroup."

Felix clicked over to the squadron channel. "All units pull back," he said.

There was no debate about who led them. Felix was the ranking pilot. Colonel Winter had reinstated him back to a full sergeant, while she'd only made Paul a corporal (reminding him how lucky he was to be out of the brig).

Something inside Ethan, though, wanted to lead. Felix was a great pilot, his friend, but Ethan always seemed to be thinking two steps ahead of him.

At the same time, Ethan was relieved *not* to be in charge. He had only a fraction of the experience and airtime, and a squadron leader was responsible for everyone's life.

Oliver, Kristov, Paul, Carl, and Lee zoomed back to their position. Madison and Emma teamed up and dove down to their level. Felix's midnight-blue beetle took a spot on Ethan's starboard wing.

Angel, though, couldn't help herself. She was spoiling for a fight. Her black wasp charged the three enemy locusts.

"No!" Ethan shouted to her.

"I got these," she called back. There was a distinct *pop* of bubblegum over the radio. The suicidal confidence in her voice was unnerving.

The jets on Paul's praying mantis flared and he raced ahead. "I'll cover her," he said.

"Don't," Felix called.

It was too late. Paul blazed toward crazy Angel, just a couple of miles from her position.

One of the locusts veered toward him.

Paul's praying mantis was quicker, snatching it right out of the air.

The locust, though, aimed for the mantis's wing. It snared a membrane and ripped it to shreds.

The two tumbled toward the ground.

Angel dove. "Hang on, Paul!" she screamed.

The two remaining locusts slammed into her black wasp. Together they fell in a ferocious ball of wrestling insect limbs and biting mandibles.

"I can't believe this!" Madison cried over the radio. "What a bunch of *idiots!*"

"Cut the chatter," Felix shouted. "We've got to save them. Follow me."

His rhinoceros beetle plummeted after them.

Ethan sighed. Couldn't Felix see it was too late? That the other Ch'zar circled above them, waiting for them to dive? From the higher altitude, they'd have a huge advantage.

The squadron was doomed. It was so obvious.

But Ethan couldn't let Felix go off alone, so, even though this was stupid, he rocketed after his friend. Orders were orders.

On the wasp's rear monitors, he spotted Madison, Emma, and the rest of the squadron charge after them.

Felix's heavy beetle fell the fastest. He kicked on his afterburners and actually caught up to Angel's black wasp as she struggled with her attackers.

The rhinoceros beetle pried off one enemy and shot at point-blank range with a particle beam, blasting it into insect confetti.

Half a mile beneath them, Paul's mantis smashed into the rocky slope of the Appalachian Mountains and blossomed into a fireball.

"Just great," Ethan muttered.

Felix and Angel hit the ground a moment later, exploded, and oily smoke plumed up from their scattered wreckage.

Ethan shook his head as, just as he'd predicted, the

mosquitoes dropped aerial bombs and rained laser fire down on what was left of the training squadron.

More locusts appeared from the clouds and zoomed in.

They'd make sure that any escaping pilots got dragged down. They'd sacrifice themselves without a thought. In theory, one Resister pilot was worth ten of them. A full Resister squadron should've been able to outthink and outfight a hundred Ch'zar.

Not today, apparently.

Oliver's heavily armored cockroach went spiraling down in flames. Madison hit her afterburners, and her dragonfly tried to climb out of the death trap. Emma struggled to stay airborne as bombs exploded around her ladybug I.C.E. Stunned, she dropped like a stone. Carl chased after her in his superagile crane fly in a valiant, but futile, attempt to save her life.

Ethan banked to engage the locusts closing on him.

Something ripped off his port-side wing.

He didn't have time to see what, because a bomb exploded in his face.

All monitors in his cockpit went blank.

"That's it!" Felix shouted. "I'm calling today's simulation."

Ethan's screens flickered to life, indicators popped from red to green, and the cockpit hatch hissed open.

He blinked. Coming out of the simulated dream state of an I.C.E. suit always took him a few moments, like waking from a dream—or in this case, a nightmare.

The other pilots emerged from their armor and stumbled onto the simulation flight deck.

Angel tore off her black gloves, wadded them, and threw them onto the ground in frustration. "This is dumb," she declared. "It's not even real!"

"Good thing, too," Madison said, her voice dripping with acid, "or you would've been splattered on the ground, burned to a crisp, *and* you would've got the rest of us killed!"

The two girls glared at each other. Madison's hands balled into fists. Angel bared her teeth like a wild animal.

Felix stepped between them, clutching his data pad in one hand like a shield. He had a slight limp, but his leg had otherwise been healed by those caterpillar bandages.

The Sterling kids gathered on one side, the Resisters on the other. Emma stood with Felix, in the middle, somehow not belonging to either group yet.

This was bad—worse even than botching today's simulation. The Ch'zar were predicted to find the Seed Bank in the next seventy-two hours. The Sterling kids and Resister pilots weren't supposed be two *separate* groups. They had to be *one* team.

Boots clipped on the flight deck behind Ethan.

He knew the stride. He turned and faced the unwavering gaze of Colonel Winter.

"I believe that is enough 'training' for one day," she said, somehow making *training* sound like *disaster*.

The kids stepped back from one another, their anger and frustration chilling in the presence of their commanding officer. Even the Sterling troublemakers backed down.

"I'm ordering everyone to get dinner and a mandatory eight hours of sleep," she said.

Angel and Madison grumbled but eventually shut up.

"Yes, ma'am," Felix said. "Come on, people." He gestured toward the exit. "Food. Sleep. It'll do everyone good."

They started to move off.

Felix sighed and glanced back at his mother, and the strength seemed to drain from his body.

Colonel Winter nodded at him, and some strength returned to Felix . . . but not all of it.

Emma hung her head and slunk off with Felix and the others.

Ethan had to cheer her up. His sister could be the glue that held them together—a Sterling refugee, almost a Resister, and maybe a better natural pilot than himself.

"A moment, Mr. Blackwood," the colonel said.

Ethan halted and his heart clenched. What was she going to chew him out for *now*?

"I've read the instructors' reports, seen the trainees' grades, and viewed the flight records," she said. "They're almost ready."

Ethan's mouth dropped open. "Almost ready? How can you say that? Tonight's simulation was a total washout, ma'am."

"True," she said, "but they're 'almost ready,' because they *have to be*. Tomorrow morning we launch a counter-assault before the Ch'zar get any closer. It will be our last chance to keep the Seed Bank hidden."

Tomorrow morning? Ethan gulped.

"There's no way they'll be ready."

Colonel Winter studied Ethan. Her iron-gray eyes never wavered, but he thought, for a microsecond, he detected a flicker of sympathy and understanding.

"Whether you know it or not, these pilots look up to *you*," she said. "You are the unacknowledged leader of this group and their inspiration. If you can't pull them together, they *will* fail tomorrow. They will die."

She held his gaze and her eyes bored into his.

Ethan struggled to find the courage not to look away

and definitely not let the prickling sensation in his eyes become full-blown tears.

"Get it done, Blackwood," she whispered, then turned on her heels and strode off.

Ethan stood there feeling helpless, suddenly holding the fate of every human on Earth in his hands.

∘ ∘ ∘ 27 ∘ ∘ ∘

SILVER BAR

ETHAN WISHED HE COULD HAVE EATEN WITH his friends in the pilots' mess. (*Mess* was the military word for "cafeteria" and had nothing to do with the state of a kitchen's cleanliness.) He also wanted to sleep. But every time he closed his eyes, he saw his sister falling through the air . . . Felix and Madison and the others all trying to save her—and dying in flames.

And every time he tried to push those thoughts from his mind, the colonel's last orders echoed in his skull— that *he* had to get them ready for tomorrow, to fly into their first, and maybe their last, battle.

So that only left one option: he hid.

Ethan had slipped away to the incubation caverns. He sat on the floor with his knees tucked up to his chest.

This was where Resister scientists raised giant insect grubs. The bugs grew and spun cocoons that solidified into a concrete-hard chrysalis as they underwent metamorphosis. The cases hung from the cave like smooth stalactites. Some were as small as garbage cans. Others were the size of trucks. Many glimmered with ghostly bioluminescent pinks, yellows, and greens. Inside, the bugs turned and shifted, restless.

Ethan figured it was the insect version of puberty.

This should have creeped him out, but instead it was warm, quiet, and, most important, peaceful in this cave.

He had just closed his eyes and relaxed when he heard footsteps.

Ethan scrunched up, hoping whoever it was didn't see him and would go away.

"So here I find you." Dr. Irving settled next to Ethan on the ground with a creaking of bones. "I thought so. I find it soothing as well. Sometimes I think I hear the metamorphosing insects gossiping with one another."

Ethan imagined it differently. To him, it seemed as if the insects sang in their sleep. He didn't understand the song but nonetheless found it comforting, like a lullaby.

"I won't pretend I know how you feel," Dr. Irving went on, adjusting his lab coat. "It must seem like the world has turned upside down since you got here and discovered part of the truth?"

Ethan exhaled. If there had to be an adult interrupting his hiding, he was glad it was Dr. Irving. He was the *one* grown-up who never gave him orders or told him he had to save the entire world.

"Wait," Ethan said. "What do you mean *part* of the truth?"

Dr. Irving turned his hands up in an apologetic gesture. "There is always more truth to know—about us, our world, what it means to be human, the good . . . and the bad parts."

Ethan already knew about the Ch'zar but sensed Dr. Irving meant something else.

"The 'bad' parts," Ethan whispered. "You're talking about *before* the aliens came. The demolished cities. The radiation in the desert. The Ch'zar didn't do that, did they?"

"No, we did," Dr. Irving said, and stared into the distance. "I did."

"How could *you* have destroyed anything?" Ethan asked with a halfhearted laugh. "You *saved* everyone here."

Dr. Irving had once told Ethan he'd built the Seed

Bank in total secrecy to save endangered species of plants and animals from the devastation of World War IV. Even the people who'd constructed the place had volunteered to stay inside to protect its hidden location. That's why the Ch'zar had never found the place when they invaded and absorbed every adult human mind on the Earth's surface. It was ironic that the most endangered species Dr. Irving had saved was free-willed humans.

"Yes, I saved everyone," Dr. Irving admitted with a dry chuckle. "But not for the reasons you think. Before that, long before, I was a boy much like you . . . and I was much different. I grew up *wanting* to be a soldier. I joined the Northern Alliance Military Academy and graduated as a pilot, top of my class. I fought for freedom, for political ideals, for land, for money, and ultimately for power."

Ethan stared at Dr. Irving until his features resolved in the dim light.

He no longer saw the face of the kindly scientist he knew. It might've been the shadows, but the wrinkles and worry lines seemed to cut deeper.

"I became the grand admiral of the air, Supreme Commander Gordon Victor Irving," he told Ethan. "They called me the Storm Falcon because I rained destruction upon the earth. I almost destroyed it *all*."

Storm Falcon? That was Dr. Irving's computer password.

Ethan remembered the broken city in Knucklebone Canyon. Dr. Irving had caused all that? Ethan refused to believe it. But the doctor had never lied to him either.

"That was the reason I created the Seed Bank," Dr. Irving explained. "I nearly burned the world to a cinder. I was responsible for so much death. It was only fitting that I atone and try to save the tiny bit of life that was left."

He sighed. The light that always sparkled in Dr. Irving's eyes was gone.

Conflicting feelings boiled inside Ethan—disgust that one person had caused so much suffering, a shred of admiration because he'd tried to make amends, and pity because Dr. Irving had had to live with the burden of his past for so long.

Ethan honestly didn't know what to think of Dr. Irving anymore. He wasn't sure this wasn't some story to distract Ethan from the upcoming battle.

Dr. Irving got to his feet with a grunt of effort. "Listen to me, talking about ancient history. I came here to help with *your* problems, not mine. Come, young man. Sitting in the dark the night before a battle is no way for leaders to act."

Dr. Irving walked out of the cavern.

Ethan jumped up and ran after him. "Hey!" he called. "What'd you mean, help me? How?"

For an old guy, Dr. Irving could walk awfully fast. He'd made it to the spiral stairs that led down to the flight deck before Ethan caught up to him.

"I could never sleep the night before a battle either," he told Ethan. "You worry about the enemy, how your pilots will do, and how you will command them in the moments they need you the most."

Dr. Irving emerged onto the flight deck.

Before them, thirty-three I.C.E. suits—the entire Resister joint squadron force—lined up in one long row: the bumblebees of Becka's Bombers, the wasps and hornets of Jack Figgin's Black and Blue Hawks, and assorted three-unit strike teams.

Ethan's wasp was there, too.

His spirits soared as he took in its freshly polished, gleaming gold-and-black armor, and its antennae perked to full alertness.

It knew a fight was coming. It was ready.

Ethan wished he felt the same way.

Tending the insects was an army of technicians, loading missiles, topping off power cells with sparking jumper cables, checking and rechecking every inch of their exoskeletons one last time.

"Nothing helps but this," Dr. Irving said. "You make sure you've done everything to prepare, and make sure that the men and women who follow you see that you're confident—because strategy rarely survives without inspiration."

For a moment, the doctor sounded so brave that Ethan believed he really had been the supreme commander of the air, the "Storm Falcon," long ago.

He should be the one out there leading the Resisters into battle.

Of course, he couldn't go. No grown-up could.

It was up to the kids.

And even though Ethan wanted to deny it, he knew it was up to him to lead.

"How can I ask anyone to follow me?" Ethan whispered. "Felix is the ranking noncommissioned officer. Even Madison, a corporal, outranks me, which is right, because I don't have a tenth of the airtime experience either of them does."

Dr. Irving held up a gnarled finger to silence him.

"Tut-tut, young man. Yes, Felix and Madison are superb pilots. Felix is an unsurpassed NCO and no doubt will be a leader one day, perhaps even leader of the Seed Bank like his mother. But who was the only neighborhood-raised child to see the truth and accept it despite years of

Ch'zar programming? Who then fought them with all his heart and won, despite overwhelming—one might even say astronomical—odds? Who stole one of our own I.C.E. wasps right under our noses and went back to try to rescue his sister from Santa Blanca? And, I might add, in doing so inspired a dozen Resister pilots to go AWOL and fight alongside him? And who broke his biggest rival out of the brig and then liberated the students of Sterling—an operation so far-fetched, no one here would have ever dared dream of it?"

Dr. Irving poked Ethan in the chest.

"You. And only you, Mr. Blackwood."

All those things were true. But none of it mattered right now.

"That doesn't mean I can lead anyone," Ethan protested. "Not into a *real* battle."

Dr. Irving ignored him. "You have a combination of talents no other pilot here has: an incredible aptitude for aerial combat, a strategic genius, and a certain disregard for authority."

Ethan hung his head.

So he'd come up with a few crazy schemes. So he'd gotten superlucky. That didn't make him a good leader. His so-called skills wouldn't be enough this time.

And yet he could see the big picture in the heat of

battle. Would that translate to seeing a good strategy when there'd be hundreds of units in the air at the same time?

"As I said," Dr. Irving told him, "nothing I can do will help with your doubts before a fight, but *this* may help with the technical command issues that have you concerned."

He reached into his lab coat pocket and took out a small black box the size of a pack of playing cards.

"Colonel Winter, her senior staff, and myself have unanimously agreed on this."

He strode to Ethan's wasp and tapped a control on one of the biomonitors. The giant wasp curled over, bending its head so its eyes were level with the doctor's. He touched the box to the wasp's black head cowl. A silver bar appeared on the center of the armor segment. It shone, reflecting the blue deck lights.

Ethan's breath caught in his throat.

He'd seen that symbol before . . . but *never* on an I.C.E. suit.

Dr. Irving then turned and touched the black box to the collar fitting of Ethan's flight suit.

The material warmed.

Ethan craned his head and pulled the fabric to see.

There was an identical, but smaller, silver bar there as well.

Dr. Irving saluted Ethan and shook his hand.

"Congratulations," Dr. Irving said, beaming at him, "on your field promotion, Second *Lieutenant* Blackwood."

Ethan was stunned speechless.

His eyes then locked onto the black box in Dr. Irving's hand, and he glanced back at the I.C.E. suits lined up on the deck, and he got an idea. He wasn't the only one who deserved special recognition.

"Just exactly how does that thing work?" Ethan asked.

∘ ∘ ∘ **28** ∘ ∘ ∘

STERLING SQUADRON

IF ETHAN HAD BUTTERFLIES BOILING IN HIS stomach before, it now felt like someone had kicked over a hornet's nest and they were attacking those butterflies. He was glad he hadn't eaten dinner, or it would've been upchucked onto the flight deck.

That'd be a *great* start to being an officer.

And it wasn't only Ethan who had a case of the nerves.

It was five in the morning, and every technician, officer, crewman, and Resister pilot crowded the flight deck of the hangar, looking worried as they wrapped up one last system check of the I.C.E. suits.

The fight was almost here.

Felix and Paul went to their armor and tried to peel off the curious bandages plastered under the wing case hinges on the insects' "shoulders." Before they could remove them, however, senior technicians waved them off the rhinoceros beetle and praying mantis.

Madison, Emma, and the other Sterling kids, also curious, asked about the bandages on their units.

However, the technicians were under Ethan's orders to say nothing about those bandages or let any pilot touch them.

It was weird for Ethan to give orders, especially to the technicians, who'd been raised at the Seed Bank, were older than Ethan, and knew encyclopedias more about I.C.E. systems.

But they'd saluted and did as he asked.

Under those bandages was a surprise Ethan had to hide from his team for just a bit longer.

Felix and Paul then noticed Ethan's wasp.

Felix's eyes widened and Paul's mouth dropped open. The boys jogged to the I.C.E. suit. They stared long and hard at the silver bar lieutenant insignia on the wasp's black head cowl.

They spotted Ethan and marched over to him.

Ethan shifted uneasily. "Hey, guys. How'd you sleep?"

"What's with the LT bar?" Paul demanded. His eyes locked onto the lieutenant insignia on Ethan's collar. "That's not possible."

Ethan reached to fold over his collar but halted. This wasn't something he should be ashamed of.

Felix shook his head, blinking, as if he'd taken a punch to his face. "It's possible," he said to Paul. "They just never *have*."

"No kid gets to be an officer," Paul whispered. "If you know that officer stuff—the codes, the security protocols—and you go outside, the Ch'zar could get you and know all that stuff, too!"

Paul was right. Ethan had never seen any kid with a rank higher than staff sergeant. And only a small fraction of the adult Resisters even got to be officers.

Felix and Paul exchanged confused glances, waiting for him to explain.

This must be what Dr. Irving had warned him about: show nothing but confidence to the people you command.

"Dr. Irving and Colonel Winter approved the promotion," he simply told them.

Paul's lips tightened into a thin white line.

Ethan figured that Paul getting reinstated as a mere private while Ethan got this huge promotion must feel like a knife stabbed into his back—painful, and just out of his reach.

"I get it," Felix said, nodding slowly and breaking the tense silence. "You've put together operations no one else here would've dared. And you giving orders simplifies things, because you've always got good ideas in the field, but, no offense . . ." Felix looked at the floor, embarrassed and unable to finish.

What he was trying to say was that Ethan didn't have the technical and practical experience to get things done in the field. No argument there from Ethan. There were a hundred I.C.E. systems Ethan wasn't familiar with, he didn't know proper first aid, and there were a million other things he figured a *real* Resister officer should know.

But they'd put Ethan in charge. He had to lead.

"That's why I'll need the best NCO here to make my crazy plans fly," Ethan said diplomatically, "which would be you, Sergeant."

Felix looked up.

An understanding passed between the two boys: Ethan would figure out the strategy, and Felix would do all the real work to get it done.

"Yeah, that ought to work," Felix whispered. He straightened and seemed relieved to not have to make the larger decisions and be responsible for everyone's lives.

"Great," Paul muttered. "Whatever. So you're the strategic wizard. You've been right about everything so far." Sarcasm dripped from his words. "I just don't have to like it, unless that's an order . . . sir."

"Feel however you like, Hicks," Ethan told him. "Just make sure you follow orders today. Our lives are going to depend on you."

Paul considered these words and finally nodded.

Just like that, the tension between the three boys evaporated.

Ethan felt a new tension take its place, though. A taut chain of military command settled into place. Paul may have almost no respect for authority, but he had *some*.

All Ethan had to do now was prove that he could lead them.

That terrified him a million times more than anything Paul could say or do to him.

"Resisters!" Colonel Winter called out, and strode across the deck.

They snapped to attention, eyes tracking her as she stopped next to Ethan.

"Here's the current situation, people," she said. "Lights."

The overhead floodlights dimmed. For a heartbeat, the only illumination was from the blue landing lights.

It made everyone look like ghosts, and it creeped Ethan out.

Holographic lasers painted the air. A model of eastern America came into focus. The view zoomed to the central Blue Ridge Mountains, with wavy lines indicating elevations.

Twitching red dots swarmed through valleys and over peaks: Ch'zar insect icons—centipedes indicating ground units and hornets indicating aerial units. There were hundreds of them. Ethan guessed those represented even more individual enemy I.C.E. units.

He swallowed. This was bad.

The Resister pilots shuffled.

Ethan felt the fear in the hangar build and the air tremble with tension.

"Our battle plan is simple and will be executed in two phases," Colonel Winter said, striding among holographic mountains like a giant.

She sounded confident, so much so that the churning in Ethan's stomach eased.

He wished he could be like that for his people. How did you *not* show fear when facing impossible odds like this?

"We are outnumbered," she told the Resisters, "but that's nothing new."

She smiled at them, the first time Ethan had seen her smile. It was a terrible, predatory grin.

Ethan was glad the colonel was on their side. The thought of *her* mind being added to the Ch'zar Collective chilled him to the core.

"The Ch'zar's mission is to find the Seed Bank," she said. "To do this, they must spread themselves over a huge region. This is a vulnerability we will exploit."

She stepped to the middle of the map.

"A command post coordinates these Ch'zar." She tapped an icon larger than the others.

It expanded into an elongated hive covered with hundreds of jointed exoskeleton limbs, artillery cannons, missile launch tubes, and tiled hexagonal armor plates. It floated among the clouds like a living zeppelin battle cruiser.

"Dr. Irving hypothesizes that with so many units in the field," she continued, "they need a mental 'booster' to direct their collective intelligence in this campaign."

Ethan gaped. The data floating next to the hologram indicated the command hive was two miles wide.

"Becka's bomber squadron will begin by saturation shelling of enemy ground units here"—she pointed to the Cumberland River Valley—"on a concentration of ant lion heavy armor."

She paused, turned, and somehow made eye contact with them all.

"This will get their attention," Colonel Winter said.

The pilots of Becka's Bombers chuckled.

"The rest of our pilots will cover the bombers as they drop into the Shawnee National Forest. We have temporarily disabled enemy satellite coverage of that region. A secret cache of bombs is hidden there for the bombers to reload. We believe the Ch'zar command hive and the balance of their high-speed units will shift position and pursue."

On the map, red arrows indicated the probable movement of the command hive and other units.

"As they give chase," she continued, "their air units will separate and spread out. Our squadrons will turn, reengage, and destroy them."

The Resister pilots nodded, seeing the strength of her strategy.

Ethan saw it, too. It was a good plan. He'd used this tactic to string out Ch'zar units a half-dozen times before.

"Our goal is to reduce their numbers so they will abandon their search mission before they locate the Seed Bank. If we crush them today, they will not try this again for a very long time."

Several Resisters clapped at this, and some shouted their enthusiasm.

Ethan saw her plan unfold in his mind: Resister bombers blowing up ground units, the Ch'zar command hive moving after them, the other Resisters mopping up the pursuing air units.

Something was wrong, though. It felt . . . off.

The colonel snapped her fingers. The overhead lights flared and washed the map away.

"Next, there is an organizational change."

She stepped behind Ethan and set her hands on his shoulders.

He did his very best not to flinch (and mostly succeeded). However, the hornets and butterflies in his stomach returned. He knew what was coming.

Ethan understood this gesture: the colonel was establishing *his* authority—literally standing behind him, backing him up.

"I'd like to present *Lieutenant* Blackwood," she declared.

Everyone—right down to the little kids who carried tools for the techs—stared at him.

Most pilots were stunned motionless. Others smiled because they'd heard rumors of Ethan's exploits. A few, though, shook their heads, only knowing Ethan Blackwood as the screwup neighborhood kid who'd nearly flunked flight training.

"Lieutenant Blackwood has field control of this operation," the colonel said. "What this means is that while the Seed Bank retains strategic control from C and C, and squadron leaders still direct their people as they see fit, the lieutenant is our intermediate. He has the authority to modify C and C's orders based on moment-to-moment battle conditions."

She let that sink in.

What this meant was that Ethan was in charge out there today.

Even in the best-case scenario, it took time for Seed Bank officers to analyze a report and issue order updates.

In an aerial dogfight, even a few seconds could mean life and death.

Rebecca Mills from Becka's Bombers, Jack Figgin of the Black and Blue Hawks, and the other team leaders of the smaller strike teams all locked eyes with Ethan.

Colonel Winter must have briefed them already and made them accept his promotion (or at least not openly complain about it) because no one protested.

"Squadron leaders," the colonel said, "get your people ready." She snapped off a crisp salute. "Good hunting to you all."

They saluted back.

Chaos erupted in the hangar as pilots swarmed to their suits and squadron leaders.

Ethan plowed through the crowds, deflected questions, and tromped to his wasp.

Next to his I.C.E. suit, the other insects in his group stood in a line. His team pushed their way toward them and gathered around Ethan.

"Lieutenant?" Emma said, grinning, and tried to punch him in the shoulder.

Ethan took a step back so she couldn't. He had to be a leader, someone you took seriously . . . not the sort of guy you punched in the shoulder.

Madison didn't comment. She just kept staring at the new rank insignia on his collar.

These people were family, like Emma. They were his friends, like Madison and Felix. One was his enemy, Paul. But most of them he hardly knew, the kids from Sterling: Angel, Kristov, Oliver, Carl, and Lee.

He'd have to give them orders today, maybe orders that would get them killed.

He wasn't sure he could do it.

They had a million questions. They were scared. He could see that. Nothing he *said* would change that.

They all needed something more than words.

Ethan signaled the technicians, and they ripped the bandages off his team's I.C.E. suits.

Underneath, bonded onto the insects' armor, was a

black triangle patch. Along its edges ran white zigzags. In the center was a bronze fist. That fist clutched the top of a large silver S.

"Our squadron's insignia," Ethan told them. "The resistors on the sides honor Madison's lost brother, who came up with the idea to use the electrical resistor as a symbol, and for all the other lost pilots."

Madison inhaled sharply and blinked away tears.

"The fist," Ethan continued, "is because we're strong and don't back down when we have to fight."

Angel seemed to like *that*, and her face brightened.

"The S stands for 'Sterling' because that's where half of us came from and because that word means something else, like a sterling character. It means excellence."

His people gazed at their squadron patch, and the weight of responsibility upon them seemed to lessen— that, or they seemed stronger and able to bear that responsibility better now with a proper symbol to inspire them.

"That's us," Ethan told them. "Sterling Squadron."

Paul stared at the patch, the doubt and sadness as he remembered Sterling crystallizing into determination on his face. "Good choice, Lieutenant," he whispered.

Ethan wanted to tell them how much he admired them—especially his sister and the rest of the Sterling kids, for getting slammed through flight training and, now, having the guts to get into I.C.E. suits and fight. He was proud of Madison and Felix for sticking with him no matter what. He was even thankful for Paul putting aside their differences to fight for the common good.

He didn't get the chance, though. Alarm Klaxons blared throughout the hangar.

"That's it!" Felix cried. "The scramble alert. Everyone mount up. Flight check and we're airborne in three minutes."

They saluted Ethan.

His squadron saluted *him*.

Ethan saluted back. He gathered his courage and told them, "Let's go kick their butts."

∘ ∘ ∘ 29 ∘ ∘ ∘

THE FAILURE OF TRIED-AND-TRUE

IT WAS JUST BEFORE DAWN. THE EASTERN edge of the world was red and jagged from the outline of the Appalachian Mountains.

They flew in formation—a huge wedge, all thirty-three Resister I.C.E.s, with Becka's Bumblebee Bombers protected in the center. The pilots cut through the air at a hundred miles an hour, each multiton insect a scant three yards from its wingmates.

Colonel Winter had ordered them to use only wing power at first to conserve jet fuel.

The air, churned by dozens of diamond-membrane

wings, sounded like the biggest thunderstorm in history rolling across the sky—so much power it rattled Ethan's bones even inside his cockpit.

Ethan felt powerful, in control, and like nothing could stop them.

It was great, but he figured it wouldn't last, so he savored the moment.

On long-range radar, he picked up scattered signals . . . everywhere.

Ch'zar aerial strike teams patrolled the mountain ridges. On the ground, centipede armor and army ant mobile infantry clear-cut forests and literally overturned every boulder searching for any 'trace of the human Resisters.

"You won't have to look for us much longer," Ethan whispered to the enemy.

He felt like he was about to play the biggest soccer match of his life. He felt like the entire human race watched him, cheered him on. He also felt like he could lose big-time.

"Incoming patrol," Madison said over the radio on a private channel. "Three mosquito scouts."

Ethan told the other squad leaders, and then said, "Take care of it."

He didn't want to give specific orders unless he absolutely had to. Better to let the squad leaders and NCOs deal with stuff like this. They had more experience at it than he did.

Ethan sensed he had to save his authority to spend at the right time . . . that, or he was just too chicken to give real orders to Resister pilots. He wasn't sure.

"I got them," said Jack Figgin of the Black and Blue Hawks.

Jack's wasps and hornets broke formation and angled toward the three scouts.

The mosquitoes must've realized that the huge shape on their radar wasn't a cloud. They banked and dove.

The Hawks filled the air with laser and particle beams, vaporizing the tiny, half-ton units. All that remained was a cloud of sparks and falling wreckage.

It was a textbook-perfect execution.

Madison broke in over the radio. "Getting readings now all over the place. *Everything* is moving."

Ethan had expected that. Three deaths in the Ch'zar collective intelligence wouldn't go unnoticed.

He wondered if there had been mind-controlled humans piloting those scouts. Maybe.

It made him queasy. He bet there'd be people in the smarter, leader-type enemy I.C.E. units. But, as much as he wanted to, Ethan couldn't let that stop him. If he hesitated, or tried to just wing the enemy, they'd use that advantage to blast the Resisters out of the air.

He didn't want to fight other humans. There was no choice, though.

If he was ever captured and absorbed into the Collective, he'd want the Resisters to keep fighting . . . even if that meant shooting *him* down.

Small comfort.

"Are they moving *toward* us?" he asked Madison.

"A few outliers veering our way," she said. "Thunderbolt locusts and some firefly sensor units. There are so many in the air, though, that could just be coincidence."

Ethan clicked on a channel to everyone. "Heat up your jets," he ordered. "Accelerate to two hundred miles an hour over the next fifteen seconds. Let's get to the Phase-One target before the enemy figures this out."

Squadron and strike team leaders acknowledged his order.

Resister I.C.E. engines flared with fire. The formation increased velocity.

Ethan had to resist the urge to pour on the speed. The heavily armored beetles would never keep up and then they'd be the ones strung out and vulnerable.

He had to think of everyone now under his command. It was nerve-racking.

Their wedge shape elongated a bit but held together as they blasted through the clouds and left swirling contrails in their thundering wake.

Ethan found he was holding his breath and forced himself to exhale. That's all he needed was to sound like a panicky little hyperventilating kid over the radio.

Angel's black wasp crept forward out of formation.

She was eager to fight. Too much so.

Ethan was about to tell her to cool it, but Felix maneuvered next to her, his rhinoceros beetle flying closer to her than was technically safe.

Her shadowy wasp slipped back into place, casually, like no one had seen her. Even always-ready-to-brawl Angel wasn't stupid enough to play bumper cars with a beetle three times her weight class.

Ethan was glad Felix had taken care of that. He could depend on his NCO.

Dead ahead was the Cumberland River Valley. Wisps of early morning fog clung to the ground. Treetops poked out and looked like a magical forest in the clouds.

His wasp's air-to-surface radar detected a thousand ant lion units on the riverbanks—some dug in, others reloading from massive earthworm armored supply crawlers.

Not that he *needed* radar to see them. There were so many ant lions that the valley glittered like it was covered with tinfoil, what they called a target-rich environment in flight school.

Ethan opened a radio channel. "Becka, it's your show," he said. "Carry out Phase One when you're ready. Jack, take your squadron. Follow and cover them. The rest of us will maintain this altitude and intercept anything that comes our way."

"Roger that," Becka replied. "Bombers line up on my vector. Ant lion artillery has a long effective vertical range, so set your drop velocity to maximum. We won't give them anything but our exhaust to shoot at."

Her squadron dropped away and their jets flared white-hot. Each bumblebee clutched a large bomb in its forelimbs. Each also had bomb racks where the pollen sacs would be on a normal bumblebee.

The bees fell, gaining speed—then their wings flared, they arced up, and they released their payloads.

The gazillion ant lions in the valley fired straight up.

The sky filled with billowing smoke and a drumroll of concussive force, but the artillery shells failed to track the near supersonic bumblebees, and the enemy projectiles all missed and dropped back to the earth.

Meanwhile, tiny wings popped from the released bombs. They swooped right and left, dodging the shells as they zeroed in on their targets.

Rows of fire erupted in the valley, like strings of fire-crackers *rat-a-tat-tatt*ing. Red and orange flowers of flame blossomed over the ground, columns of earth exploded skyward, and a haze of silver armor shrapnel sparkled and then vanished in a blanket of boiling black smoke.

Every Resister pilot gave a victory scream and cheered. They'd creamed them!

"Regroup on me," Ethan said in a calm, authoritative voice.

He raced ahead to where Becka's Bombers would climb back to their altitude.

"Madison" he said, "situation report."

"*That* got their attention!" she told him. "Tracking over a hundred fast-attack hornets angling toward us. Their command hive is turning, too."

Excitement made her words quaver. Or was that tension and fear?

Ethan couldn't let *his* fear get the better of him. They'd all pick up on it.

But that wasn't easy.

Ethan watched as vast numbers of Ch'zar air units pulled together like a huge storm cloud. From this darkening thunderhead, a line streamed toward them, hundreds of crazed bugs intent on ripping them to pieces.

Now the *real* fight began.

Ethan had to time it just right, waiting until the faster enemies spread out, but not before the slower moving reinforcements could catch up or before the artillery on that floating hive got them in range and zeroed in on their position.

"Jack, take your Hawks and form on Sterling's port side," Ethan ordered. "Strike teams Comet and Scimitar, on our starboard edge. We'll throttle up and burn a path through the forward enemy units. All other teams will take out stragglers—except Team Lancelot. I want you to escort the bombers while they reload."

The channels were silent.

There wasn't a single complaint or questioning of his orders.

Ethan was in control. For the first time today, he thought maybe they could win this.

The line of attacking Ch'zar units slowed.

Something was off.

"Stand by," Ethan told his pilots.

He felt the same "offness" he'd experienced when the colonel had briefed them on her plan.

This should've worked. These were tried-and-true, familiar tactics.

But for some reason *that* bothered Ethan, too.

The Ch'zar fast-attack hornets curved and banked

back to their command hive. The balance of the enemy's slower I.C.E. suits formed up—but *not* to engage the Resisters.

They instead spread in a fan shape, dove ground side, in the *other* direction.

"What's going on?" Felix whispered to Ethan on a private channel.

"Just a second," Ethan whispered back. "Don't let anyone break formation. This might be a trick. . . ." His voice trailed off and his brain went into overdrive trying to figure this out.

What were they doing?

Not attacking. Obviously.

But why?

The Resister bombing run should've gotten their attention. The tactic had worked a bunch of times before. Hadn't Madison and Felix told him that once the Ch'zar's collective intelligence made up its mind, they almost never changed it?

Come to think of it, this diversion-and-draw-out tactic was the same one Ethan had used at Sterling. He'd done something to get their attention and then done the opposite of what they'd expected—the initial Ward Zero escape, the school riot, and then going *back* to rescue Felix.

It then clicked into place in his brain.

Ethan knew exactly what was going on . . . exactly what was wrong.

The adrenaline in his blood cooled and felt like ice crackling up his veins, half paralyzing him with fear.

Colonel Winter broke in over his radio's command channel. "Blackwood! What are you waiting for? Engage the enemy. Take out their lead attack units."

"There won't be lead attack units," Ethan told her. "They're circling back. The plan won't work."

They were going to lose this battle.

The Ch'zar would find the Seed Bank.

If they didn't die today, every Resister would lose their minds to the alien Collective.

And Ethan knew it was his fault.

∘ ∘ ∘ 30 ∘ ∘ ∘

∩EW TACTICS

FOUR LARGE MISSILES LAUNCHED FROM THE
floating Ch'zar command hive. They billowed smoke and
rocketed toward the Resisters.

"Orders?" Felix asked Ethan over the radio, his voice
crackling with tension.

"Hold this course," Ethan told him. "Everyone target
the incoming projectiles and fire from here."

"That's a tough shot," Paul said. "Those missiles are
moving at Mach speeds."

"I know," Ethan replied. "Just hit them."

"Roger that."

They held position and their weapons made the air waver from the energy buildup.

They fired.

The air lit with near-parallel brilliant red and dazzling blue beams.

Sweat trickled down Ethan's back. He gripped his controls tighter. He got his target lock rings to overlap on-screen on one incoming missile. He fired his wasp's laser. The tip of the enemy missile heated to dull red.

"Lieutenant, report!" Colonel Winter shouted.

"Hang on," Ethan told her, and double-checked the encryption on his radio channel. He didn't trust that the Ch'zar weren't listening in.

Still guiding his laser at the incoming missile, Ethan said to the colonel, "This is my fault. I fooled the Ch'zar in Santa Blanca and at Sterling and so many other times. Now they've made up their collective mind to *expect* a trick!"

There was silence on the channel as the colonel considered this.

"Go on," she said.

The missiles roared toward the Resisters. The one Ethan painted in his sights exploded. Then another prematurely blasted to bits. And another.

The last one, though, corkscrewed, and no one had a target lock on the thing as it closed in on them.

"They've finally learned to *learn from us*," Ethan whispered. "They're not taking the bait this time. In fact, they're moving *away* from the selected bombing target."

Toward the Seed Bank.

He didn't say this, but it had to be.

Colonel Winter would have only picked a target that drew the enemy farther from the base. The Ch'zar had guessed the Resisters' misdirection ploy . . . and so concentrated their search efforts in the opposite direction.

"Understood," the colonel said. "We're formulating a new plan. In the meantime, Lieutenant, take care of them. Command out."

The channel went dead.

Take care of them?

Did she mean "take care of them" as in take the Ch'zar out?

Or did she mean "take care of them" as in the pilots? As in retreat and live to fight another day?

That last corkscrewing missile loomed large on his view screens.

It blasted through their formation and exploded in their midst.

Ethan slammed into the side of his cockpit. Sparks shot from control panels, black stars filled his head, and every monitor blanked . . . and then flickered back on.

A bronze hornet and cobalt-blue wasp spiraled from their ranks toward the ground, leaking hydraulic fluid and smoking. The hornet's pilot ejected and a parachute popped open. The I.C.E. wasp fluttered its wings and made it to the ground. Those were Jack Figgin's people.

"Units three and five on my wing," Jack shouted over the radio. "We're going down to get them."

"Belay that order," Ethan said. (*Belay* was the military term that meant "stop.") "We need to stay up here, all of us, or we'll get picked apart."

Two pilots on the ground. Ethan shuddered. He wouldn't wish that on anyone with the earth literally crawling with thousands of Ch'zar infantry units. Those downed pilots would be killed—or worse, captured.

Another volley of missiles erupted from the Ch'zar carrier. The enemy I.C.E. units hung back and didn't engage, letting the hive blast Ethan's forces to bits.

"What do we do?" Paul screamed. "We can't just stay and take this punishment!"

There was an edge of mutiny in Paul's voice.

Ethan didn't blame him. He was blowing it. They were outnumbered, outgunned, and the Ch'zar had adapted to his tactics.

Ethan had to come up with *new* tactics, ones that *no*

one would predict. Easier said than done. How did you fool someone who'd learned all your tricks?

The answer came to him in a flash. It was so simple.

You fooled someone who'd learned all your tricks by *not* tricking them.

If, for example, this were a soccer game, he would turn around and try to make a straight rush for the goal. The Ch'zar wouldn't be expecting *that* because it was totally nuts, but Ethan would have one last trick up his sleeve for them.

His excitement faded, though, as he realized what that last trick was going to cost him.

"Stand by," Ethan told them in a steady voice. "I have to plan."

Rebecca from the bomber squadron broke through. "We're about to descend to the reload point, Lieutenant. Do we abort and get back there?"

"Negative," Ethan told her. "Continue with the original orders. Reload as fast as you can. We're going to need those bombs."

Ethan's voice rose in pitch with panic. He cleared his throat. He couldn't fall apart now, not when his people needed him the most.

He stared at the incoming missiles. They *all* had corkscrew trajectories this time.

So the Ch'zar *had* learned to learn.

"Break formation on my mark," Ethan told his pilots. "Scatter pattern omega."

The missiles tore through the air, getting nearer, so close now Ethan saw organic vein patterns along their sleek bodies.

"Break!" he shouted.

The I.C.E. suits in formation jetted off in a dozen directions.

The missiles veered back and forth, trying to track them all.

Two missiles bumped together, tumbled, detonated, and spilled a chain of fire across the air.

The other missiles piled into those explosions and blasted themselves into bits of metal.

"Form strike teams," Ethan said. "Clear the airspace of straggler enemies, and then close on the units near that carrier."

The Resister pilots broke and engaged enemy locusts, wasps, and beetles that hadn't joined the rest of the Ch'zar fleet and had been hovering just out of effective weapons range.

To the Ch'zar, this would look like a desperate attempt from the Resisters to win . . . or set up some sort of trick.

Which is exactly what it was—only this time, a misdirection of Ethan's *true* misdirection.

"Felix, Emma, and Madison," Ethan said. "I need you with me. Fall back."

"But I can fight," Emma protested. "Don't you dare keep me out just because I'm your sister!"

Ethan admired her courage. If only he *could* keep her safe . . .

An enemy hornet flashed right in front of Ethan—with amber-and-black exoskeleton plates and an armor-piercing stinger.

His wasp barrel-rolled out of a fatal collision at the last second and then gave chase, jets firing to catch the hornet without Ethan even giving the command.

Ethan pulsed his laser and shot the insect at point-blank range—through and through, tail to head.

"I'm not taking *anyone* out of this fight," Ethan shouted back to his sister. "Madison, climb to forty thousand feet, scan everything and give team leaders updates every thirty seconds."

"Roger," Madison replied.

Ethan watched her dragonfly blast into a steep, graceful ascent. He hoped it wasn't the last time he saw her, but it very well might be.

"Emma," Ethan said, "you and Felix move with me fifteen miles west and climb to thirty thousand."

"There are no enemies there," Felix said, confused.

"I know," Ethan said. "Trust me."

A lump wedged in Ethan's throat. He'd just gotten his sister back. The thought of losing Emma again paralyzed him.

He couldn't do this.

But he couldn't *not* do it either, because if they lost this battle, he'd lose Emma anyway.

Ethan had to order his sister and his best friend on a suicide mission.

"I'm sending you both in," he said, "to destroy that Ch'zar hive."

∘ ∘ ∘ 31 ∘ ∘ ∘

IF WE DON'T SPLATTER...

ETHAN, EMMA, AND FELIX HOVERED ON the sidelines of the battle. Felix's rhinoceros beetle and Emma's killer ladybug had such powerful wingbeats to keep their heavy units aloft that the turbulence buffeted Ethan's light (just three tons) wasp like a feather.

They waited and watched.

It drove Ethan nuts. He felt like a fake—like people thought he was out here doing nothing because he didn't know what to do.

The other Resister pilots had got drawn in closer to

the Ch'zar command hive. They dove and rolled and fought the Ch'zar units that protectively encircled it.

The enemy hadn't fired more big missiles. Maybe the Resister pilots were too close to the hive and the Ch'zar would risk damaging themselves.

A lucky break.

From fifteen miles out, all Ethan could see were tiny puffs of plasma and bursts of fire and laser light. He heard his pilots, though, like they were right next to him. Over the open radio channel, a flood of voices shouted, *"Watch out! . . . Roll to port. . . . Three on your tail! . . . Yeah, got one! No, pull back! . . . Starboard wing is shredded."*

His pilots were the best fliers, but they couldn't last much longer.

They had to, though—long enough to make the Ch'zar think this was their real, crazy plan.

Not the *other* crazy plan Ethan had up his sleeve.

"Station-keeping formation," Ethan told Felix and Emma.

The rhinoceros beetle and ladybug hovered closer to his wasp. Sunlight glinted off their shells, midnight blue and ruby red. Ethan flashed a tiny laser beam to them. It was a secure command channel. No one else could eavesdrop.

"What are we doing out here?" Emma shouted. "What did you mean we have to take out that command hive?"

"Everything depends on surprise," Ethan told her. "Colonel Winter said the Ch'zar need that command hive to keep their collective intelligence working with so many units out here. If we destroy it, I think the enemy I.C.E. units will revert to their native insect intelligence. They'll still be deadly, but then we can at least outthink them."

"Sure," Emma said. "We'll just fly up to their hive, knock on their front door, and ask them to fly it into a volcano."

"Sarcasm aside," Felix added, "your sister has a point. That thing is too big and has too much armor for our weapons to do any real damage."

"It's not armored on the *inside*," Ethan told them.

"Of course not," Emma said. "But how does *that* help?"

Ethan looked up. The three of them were lined up and staring straight down the front of the Ch'zar command hive.

"We're going to make a run at the nose," Ethan told them. "We'll link up and use our jets to build velocity fast. I'll go in partway and use all my fuel to boost you two."

"Why us?" Emma asked, now suddenly deadly serious . . . and scared.

"You two have the heaviest armor in our group," Ethan explained. "You have the best chance to puncture the outer skin."

"*If* we don't splatter on their armor first, and *if* we get in," Felix said with growing enthusiasm as he caught on to Ethan's insane scheme, "our suits have full racks of missiles and heavy particle beams. We'll be able to do some *real* damage to that thing!"

"And then die?" Emma whispered.

"Not necessarily." Ethan's heart felt ready to burst, but he went on, managing to sound halfway in control of his fear. "I'm going to order the Resisters to hit the hive's nose and tail, soften it up at the last moment. Hopefully those parts will be damaged enough so you and Felix can punch inside, unload your missiles, and have enough momentum to punch back out."

Even to Ethan this sounded far-fetched.

"There's one thing that'll help," he continued. "Dr. Irving told me that the Ch'zar technology we borrow for our I.C.E. suits flexes the molecular structure of their outer surfaces. It momentarily makes them superstrong. You're going to need to keep your minds focused on the leading edges of your bugs. You can make them tougher than titanium—harder than diamond."

"I don't know . . . ," Felix whispered.

Ethan had sympathy for his sister and his friend.

But they couldn't afford doubt.

"There's nothing *to* know," Ethan said to Felix. "It's our only chance. And it's an order."

There was silence from Emma and Felix.

Emma finally replied, "The colonel said you were in charge, Ethan, but that doesn't matter to me. What matters is that you came back to Santa Blanca to rescue me. You came to Sterling to rescue us all. I know you wouldn't do this unless we needed to. And you wouldn't do it unless we had at least a chance of surviving." Her voice hitched in her throat. "I trust you."

"So do I," Felix added apologetically. "You've been right so far. Even about the *crazy* stuff."

Ethan was dying inside because he didn't believe in himself half as much as they did, but he kept all the doubts and fears to himself. Like Dr. Irving had told him, *Make sure that the men and women who follow you see that you're confident, because strategy rarely survives without inspiration.*

Ethan *had* to be strong. For Emma. For Felix. For everyone.

Paul shouted over the radio, "Ethan? We're getting creamed out here. Do something!"

Ethan switched to the normal channel. "Resisters, stand by for new orders in approximately one minute."

He stretched out his wasp's forelimbs to Emma's ladybug and the rhinoceros beetle. "Let's link up and do this."

Emma hesitated and then reached out with her ladybug. Felix took her "hands" and then Ethan's. The insects had tiny barbed hooks on their limbs that interlocked like Velcro.

Ethan wished he could hug his sister and shake Felix's hand, for real, just once more.

But, of course, they had to stay in their suits.

Jet engines popped from his wasp's sides and flared to life. Larger engine intakes and exhaust ports *thunk*ed open on the ladybug and the rhinoceros beetle and roared with thunder.

Their wings buzzed and then locked in place as their combined jet thrust overcame their inertia. They propelled toward the Ch'zar command hive.

Acceleration squished Ethan into the back of his cockpit, the skin on his face stretched and his vision blurred.

He held on tight to the controls and steered toward the fast-growing target on his central screen.

Head-on, the armored floating hive looked like a giant bull's-eye.

"Brace for impact," he said, "in sixty seconds. . . ."

○ ○ ○ 32 ○ ○ ○

END IN FIRE

IT WAS LIKE RIDING A ROCKET—ONE OF those models Ethan and his sister had loved to shoot off last year.

Back in Santa Blanca, they'd built rockets. Ethan had made the boosters with his junior chemistry set. Emma had constructed the body and fins from epoxy and cardboard tubes. Together they launched them up into the clouds. Some they never found (and Ethan imagined they'd gone into orbit). It was great!

Until they'd accidentally shot one into their neighbor's open garage.

He and Emma had been marched before the School Board of Ethical Behaviors. Ethan had thought that'd be the worst trouble he'd ever get into.

Boy, had he been wrong.

Ethan called over his command channel, "Jack, take your squadron and hit the nose of that hive with everything you've got! Everyone else destroy the tail!"

His pilots were brilliant. It was as if they all woke up and *really* started fighting. They blasted the enemy I.C.E. units dogfighting them and sped toward their new targets.

Jack's squadron hit the nose with particle beams and missiles. So much raw destruction poured out of the insects that they almost looked like they were on fire.

The brand-new pilots of Sterling Squadron—Angel, Kristov, Carl, Lee, and Oliver—zoomed toward the back and let loose with lasers, ripping to shreds the last enemy I.C.E. suits that got in their way.

The Ch'zar hive also woke up, though.

Laser cannons suddenly bristled from the hive's surface and heated.

Resister pilots rolled to avoid the beams, but Ethan spotted at least one of his units flame out and plummet to the ground.

The artillery mounted on the top of the hive swiveled, tracked Ethan, Emma, and Felix, and fired at them!

Plumes of smoke curled from the artillery muzzles. Blurred shells, friction-heated and red-hot, hurled straight toward them.

Ethan felt a huge explosion tear through his body.

He was dead.

Or at least that's what he thought for a split second.

On the radio, Emma yelled over the shell-rattling noise, "Mach one!"

That was a sonic boom—*their* sonic boom! They'd broken the sound barrier.

Ethan jammed his afterburners to maximum, dumping all his fuel into one cataclysmic thrust.

The good news was that they were going so fast they'd be impossible to track and hit.

The bad news was they were going so fast they were going to slam into the enemy hive at supersonic speeds.

Felix shouted, "Your wasp's armor can't survive the impact. Get off, Ethan!"

Ethan had three more seconds of fuel to contribute to their forward thrust.

"Not yet!" he shouted back.

"Yes, now," Felix said, and his rhinoceros beetle shoved Ethan. "You have to lead everyone."

Emma pushed him off, too.

Before Ethan could get a grip, he tore free and

tumbled into the air . . . reaching helplessly after his sister and his friend.

They were gone.

His wasp spun so fast it felt as if it were going to fly apart.

He hit the emergency controls and snapped the wasp's wings flat against its body. He pulled back and got the head up, using the bug's aerodynamic surfaces to stabilize his tumble.

Emma and Felix were already miles away. Ethan's afterburners and them jettisoning him had effectively given them a huge push forward—straight toward the nose of the Ch'zar hive.

There, the armored plates were pockmarked, smoldering from fresh laser fire, and in a few spots falling off. The Resisters had done a good job.

Would it be enough?

Emma's ladybug and Felix's beetle hit.

And vanished.

There were no explosions. No fireballs.

One moment they rocketed toward the hive—the next there was a crater, curled inward, its edges white-hot and boiling.

"They're inside!" Ethan cried, and whooped. "All

Resisters, pull back and prepare to repel massive Ch'zar reinforcements."

His wasp hurtled past the hive, his momentum still too great to control with wings alone.

The side of the command hive bulged, and a jet of fire flared from one small tear.

That had to be Emma and Felix, shooting missiles and beams at the enemy hive—*from the inside.*

Which meant they were still alive!

Ethan exhaled, relieved; then he thought of another possibility and his insides turned icy cold. Or it meant they'd hit something their suits couldn't punch through . . . and all their onboard missiles had detonated at once.

Dents popped out over the Ch'zar hive's skin, bubbling toward the tail section as if someone were making popcorn in there, beating the inner surfaces with rapid-fire impacts.

Ethan suddenly hit the sound barrier with a teeth-grinding decelerating jerk.

His velocity gauge shuddered at seven hundred miles an hour. He snapped his wings open and banked back to get a better look.

Explosions ripped through the tiny tears in the hive's skin. Fire and lightning arced across the structure. The tail detonated and house-sized chunks of metal and exoskeleton spun through the sky. Clouds of oily smoke streamed out.

The hive tilted and drifted to the ground.

"Emma!" he cried over radio. "Felix! Report."

Static flooded their radio channels.

"Madison, come in," Ethan said. "Do you see anything up there?"

High above the battle, Madison's dragonfly circled. "There were too many objects falling from the hive for me to pick out any single units," she said. "No emergency transponder signals either. I'm sorry, Blackwood. I can't tell if they're alive or . . ."

Madison choked up. She couldn't say it.

Ethan imagined Emma and Felix caught inside that Ch'zar hive.

He watched the hive hit the ground, deflate, and collapse. Pillars of fire erupted and sent spirals of superheated gas skyward that turned into a storm of sparks and thick black smoke.

They'd burn if they were in there.

Or just maybe they'd punched all the way through and made it out, where they could be lying broken and bleeding among the scattered debris.

"One more thing," Madison said. "Every enemy unit within a hundred miles is closing on your position."

"Great," he murmured.

"Resisters," he called over his command channel. "This is it. We have to win. No matter what."

"Roger that," Jack replied. "Hawk Squadron ready."

"Sterling Squadron itching to tear them apart, sir," Paul said.

Other voices chimed in over the radio: *"Good to go, sir. . . . We'll stomp 'em flat, Lieutenant. . . . They don't stand a chance! . . . Just getting warmed up here, Blackwood."*

"Regroup on my wasp," he said.

The Resister's I.C.E. suits swarmed around him. They were battered, leaking ichor, weapons depleted, and antennae broken, but right now Ethan thought the hideous giant bugs were the most beautiful things in the world.

So many feelings churned inside him.

Fear mostly.

But pride, too, for the Resister pilots.

He was worried for Emma and Felix . . . for all of them, really.

Mostly, though, Ethan was resolute. They couldn't lose this. If they did, they'd *become* the enemy. He wouldn't let that happen. Forget the odds. He'd go down swinging—even die rather than lose himself to the aliens who'd taken his world.

The enemy flew in from every direction, so many I.C.E. units that the skies looked misty, then overcast, then solid black. They came over the mountains, up from the forests, and spiraling from the river valleys: locusts, mosquitoes, bees, praying mantises, beetles, assassin bugs, damselflies, and dragonflies.

Instead of engaging the Resisters, though, they dove down to the wounded Ch'zar command hive.

They dug through the wreckage—many enemy bugs catching fire in the process—but they searched and ripped through the hull of the downed structure.

Ethan couldn't believe it. What were they doing?

"Stand by, Resisters," Ethan whispered.

Facing overwhelming numbers, a hundred Ch'zar fliers for every one of them, even fight-happy Angel didn't dare budge out of formation.

What could be so important to get off that hive that the Ch'zar would order their *own* units to burn alive to do it? When every Ch'zar knew everything the others knew? No single individual in the Ch'zar Collective was *that* important.

Or were they?

What if a Ch'zar—a *real* Ch'zar, one of the aliens who actually had come to Earth—was on that thing?

Maybe the Ch'zar were willing to throw away their human slaves, but he bet they'd do anything to save themselves.

That had to be it.

And Ethan knew how he could draw more of the enemy bugs to their doom.

"Becka," he whispered. "Move your bombers in, line up, and blast that thing to smithereens! Nothing fancy—just get down there fast. Everyone else, follow and cover them."

"Roger that, Lieutenant," she said.

The bomber bumblebees rolled and dove.

Ethan fell alongside them with the rest of the Resisters. Any enemy unit that even looked up, they flashed with lasers, launched missiles, and blasted before they took to the air.

The bombers released their payloads only a thousand feet over the hive carrier—the big blockbusters and dozens of the smaller incendiary bombs from their "pollen" sacs.

They pulled out of the dive.

Ethan had a hard time, having used up his jet fuel. He had wings, and that was it, to stay aloft.

Flashes and fire splashed over the ground. Napalm and lightning-bright thermite blanketed the hive. Everything was incinerated.

Ethan wobbled and faltered at five hundred feet.

The external temperature read over 650 degrees Fahrenheit, hot enough to melt lead. It was getting too toasty inside the cockpit to even touch the controls.

Ethan rolled out of the rising pillar of boiling heat before he was roasted alive.

Below him, a huge swath of the Daniel Boone National Forest blazed.

A few sagging struts of the carrier hive's exoskeleton stuck up but were slowly melting to slag. Enemy insects still dug through wreckage on the ground, on fire, limbs burning and turning to ash, so focused on their task that they didn't even realize they were getting cooked.

More enemy bugs landed and kept searching . . . and dying.

Ethan watched, astonished.

He felt sick, remembering that it wasn't only the enemy down there in those I.C.E. suits, but also human slaves. Ex-Sterling kids.

If there had been a real Ch'zar in the fire, he was glad. They'd killed one of the *real* enemy today. Maybe they'd think twice about fighting the Resistance again.

That thought nearly struck him dumb.

Did that mean they'd *won*?

He was still alive. Still Ethan Blackwood.

He shook. Tears blurred his eyes and poured down his cheeks.

Then he remembered Felix and Emma and fumbled for the radio.

Felix's voice crackled over the radio first. "Ethan! Lieutenant!"

"Felix? You made it? Thank goodness! Where's Emma?"

"She's okay—with me," Felix replied. "We're on the ground, but I think we're going to need *matching* casts this time."

○ ○ ○ 33 ○ ○ ○

A NEW MISSION

ETHAN STRODE THROUGH THE SEED BANK hospital ward. The walls had self-heating glow tiles that made it feel like a warm sunny day even deep underground. The acting NCO of Sterling Squadron, Corporal Madison J. Irving, walked by his side, her head held high.

He was glad Madison was here. When he'd climbed out of his wasp, he'd shaken so badly he could barely stand. In front of Madison, though, Ethan had been able to stuff his fear deep down and look reasonably normal (although he still felt as if he shook on the inside).

Ethan and Madison pushed through the door to the

recovery ward, and he caught the sharp scent of antiseptic alcohol, a honeysuckle odor from those gross caterpillar bandages, and, of course, from the rows of beds, the smell of blood and singed hair.

So many Resister pilots had been hurt but kept fighting, obeying Ethan's orders.

He stopped at Paul's bedside.

"You okay?" he asked Paul.

Paul lifted his caterpillar-wrapped arm. "A little burn," he said. "Nothing I can't handle. The mantis is going to need serious work, though." He tried to brush his sandy hair out of his face but couldn't with the bandaged limb. He smiled. "Let's do it again sometime, Lieutenant."

Ethan shook his head. "I don't think so."

Madison fussed over Paul, brushing the hair from his face and fluffing a pillow for him.

Ethan knew it was going to be okay between Paul and him. Paul would always hate him a little. He'd forever be pushing to see who was the better pilot (Ethan was), but they weren't to-the-death rivals anymore, and he'd follow Ethan's orders. They were both Resisters fighting the same enemy.

Ethan patted Paul on the shoulder, just hard enough to make him wince.

He and Madison marched down the ward to check on the others.

Paul thankfully hadn't asked the one thing Ethan couldn't talk about. If he had, the fear bottled inside him would have bubbled up. He'd lose it. Ethan would have cried in front of everyone.

Only, lieutenants didn't cry in front of the pilots under their command.

He and Madison visited pilots with busted fingers and arms, with minor internal injuries from the bruising acceleration of the protracted dogfight, a few with cracked skulls, and so many with laser and plasma burns.

Ethan clasped their hands and had encouraging words for all, but every time he bolstered *their* faith in the Resistance, a bit of *his* melted away.

Was this what being an officer meant?

Geez, he was only second lieutenant. How did Colonel Winter deal with the pressure? How had Dr. Irving survived being grand admiral of the air and supreme commander?

Ethan guessed because they *had* to. You did whatever it took to survive in a war.

He and Madison finally came to Angel's bed.

He knew he had to face the big question. If not for himself, then for her.

Sitting by her bedside were the rest of the Sterling kids: Kristov, Oliver, and Lee. They stood as Ethan neared. Even Angel sat up straighter.

"At ease," he told them.

Ethan would never get used to that. It made him feel like he wasn't one of them anymore.

Angel's black wasp I.C.E. had got a wing singed when she blasted a chunk off the hive's tail. The wing could be regrown, but it'd taken her out of the fight.

She'd landed, and Carl had dropped to the ground to make sure she was okay.

A stray shell from ant lion artillery had ripped open Carl's suit. Resister search-and-rescue teams never found his body.

Carl, the boy who'd first greeted them in Ward Zero in a hospital gown, was missing in action. He was one of three pilots who, in all likelihood, had been taken by the Ch'zar.

They'd accelerate the puberty processes in those kids and absorb them into the Collective. They'd make them fight for the enemy. They'd *be* the enemy.

Angel looked into Ethan's face. The crazy gleam was gone from her eyes.

"Doctors told me I tore a few ligaments from the rough landing," she said. "Nothing that'll take me out of the fight for long."

It sounded like a fight, though, was the last thing she wanted now.

They stared at one another for a long moment. Her cracked lips parted, and she tried to get words out but couldn't.

She couldn't ask the question that was on everyone's mind: Were Carl and the other pilots gone for good? Was there *any* hope that the kids, the adults, any human the Ch'zar had taken could come back?

"A few days ago," Ethan said, "they told me it'd be impossible to break into Sterling and rescue anyone. A few days ago, I thought the Ch'zar had my sister and I'd never see her again. And a few days ago, the enemy was about to find the Seed Bank and wipe us out."

He made eye contact with all the kids (this was the same thing Colonel Winter did when she gave a speech). "We turned it around," he said. "Made the impossible, possible. We'll get our people back. All of them."

Angel nodded. A tear trickled down her cheek. She didn't sob, didn't look sad. Instead, she looked ready to fight again . . . and not because she loved to fight. She had a reason now.

"Get better," Ethan whispered to her, and moved on.

Inside, he shook a tiny bit less.

Did he believe his own words? He wasn't sure. Yes. Some. Maybe.

He and Madison then marched to Felix and Emma's private room.

Those two rated their own room because everyone had been mobbing them with congratulations and questions, and neither of the two heroes of the battle had gotten *any* rest.

Madison grabbed Ethan's hand and pulled him to a halt just outside their door.

"Are you going to be okay?" she asked, biting her lower lip. "I mean, if I had to order Felix and my own sister to do something so dangerous . . ." She looked at the floor, unable to meet his eyes. "I don't think I could've."

Ethan appreciated her concern. He *did* feel guilty for ordering Felix and Emma on that suicide run. He would have felt worse, though, if he hadn't and they'd all died.

But for some reason it seemed like it was Madison who needed the comforting.

Ethan squeezed her hand once and let go. He started to put his hand on her slender shoulder like he would've for Felix or Paul, a gesture of camaraderie, but that felt wrong with her. There was a static electricity that crackled between them. It was more than the close friendship between two pilots. It might've been all that going-to-dances, dating, boy-girl stuff.

Ethan broke out in a sweat. If so, it'd have to wait.

He was her commanding officer, and that complicated something that already felt more complicated than advanced algebra to him.

"I'd do it again if I had to," Ethan whispered. "Ordering Emma and Felix in was the only chance we had."

"Yeah, I get that," she said. "But do *they* know that?"

Ethan took in a deep, shuddering breath. "Let's find out."

He pushed through the swinging door.

Felix had one leg propped up in a cast. He'd rebusted the same leg he'd broken at Sterling. He also had a caterpillar cast on his right arm—elbow to wriggling thumb.

In the bed next to him, Emma had a cast, too, but on her left arm.

They looked like bookends.

"You'll pardon me, sir, if I don't salute," Felix said, and a broad smile spread over his bruised face.

"Hey, little brother," Emma said. "About time you got down to visit us. Did you bring me a magazine to read or maybe a pencil so I can scratch under this cast? It's driving me crazy."

His sister had a black eye, but her nose scrunched and her freckles seemed to dance as she laughed.

This was the next best thing to coming home. Emma, Madison, and Felix were Ethan's family now.

"You two are lucky," Ethan told them with mock seriousness. "The doctor said you get to slack for another week. We're slaving away repairing the I.C.E. suits. So don't try to milk this 'busted bone' thing too long, okay?"

"Forget that." Emma swung her legs over the side of her bed. "I'm good to go now! I want to see my ladybug."

The swinging door burst inward and nearly flattened Ethan and Madison, who jumped out of the way at the last second.

Colonel Winter and Dr. Irving entered. The colonel took in the room and pinned Emma with her famous cast-iron glare.

"Your doctor has ordered bed rest, Miss Blackwood," the colonel told her. "I suggest you follow those orders. It would be a shame to have to finish your recovery in the brig."

"Yes, ma'am!" Emma yelped, and jumped back into bed.

Dr. Irving whispered to Ethan, "Well done, young man. Your performance on the battlefield was superb. I couldn't have done better."

Ethan nodded and cleared his throat. He wasn't sure how to address Dr. Irving. Was he still the grand admiral of the air? Did that mean he ordered the colonel around?

"I'm glad I caught you all together," the colonel said. "There's much to discuss."

Ethan figured this would be a speech about how brave they were. He hoped she had medals for Emma and Felix. Maybe she'd take away his promotion—say it was a temporary thing, which would be annoying, but also a huge relief.

The colonel moved to Felix's bed and sat. She tapped his arm cast and made the caterpillar squirm. "One more broken bone? You're going to catch up to my record soon if you're not careful."

Felix gave her a half smile. "Don't worry, Mom. It only hurts when I move it."

"Well"—she stood—"I'll order calcification treatments to accelerate your healing. I'll need you in the field as soon as possible."

She took out her tablet computer and flashed it toward them. On-screen was a map of North America.

The red splotches that had once converged on the Appalachian Mountains were gone. There were still a few insect icons here and there on the East Coast, but nothing like before.

"Doctor?" The colonel handed him the tablet.

Dr. Irving tapped on the screen. "This is a simulation of Ch'zar insect population growth, based on our latest updated numbers."

At first nothing happened.

The red splotches then divided and multiplied and there were hundreds of them again.

"This is within two months," Dr. Irving said. "The enemy has developed new incubation hives on the East Coast specifically to counter our efforts."

Colonel Winter cupped her chin, deep in thought, and started to pace.

"But we won . . . ," Ethan whispered.

The colonel stopped pacing. "We won for today," she said. "But the Ch'zar will be back. They have learned to learn from their mistakes. Next time they will hit us with more units. They'll start searching closer to the Seed Bank's true location. They'll increase the defenses of any command hive they send in. They *will* find us—it is only a matter of time."

Silence blanketed the room. The only sounds were the bleeps from the biomonitors on Emma and Felix (which noticeably sped up as the colonel explained the situation).

"We have a new mission for you and your squadron, Ethan," Dr. Irving said.

"If we can't fight and win next time," the colonel said, "we need you to find a location for a new Seed Bank." She grabbed the tablet from Dr. Irving and shoved it at Ethan.

His hands felt numb, but he somehow took the tablet without dropping it and stared at it.

He had to find them a new base?

Colonel Winter gazed at him with absolute confidence. That's what Dr. Irving had told him a *real* commander had to look like. Inspirational.

Ethan then looked to Dr. Irving. He couldn't read the sparkle in his eyes.

"You know what you have to do, Ethan," Dr. Irving whispered.

Ethan gulped and tapped on the map, zooming in on the Great Western Desert region.

There might be other bases out there, older military bases from World War IV—before the Ch'zar came and conquered Earth.

"Here." Ethan traced the edge of the radiation zones. "Near the big old cities. Just on the edge where it's safe. The Ch'zar won't be there."

Dr. Irving nodded.

The colonel was right. The Ch'zar had learned how to learn (thanks to him). His tricks wouldn't work next time. The Seed Bank would eventually be destroyed. The only hope for the Resistance was to not be here when they next showed up.

He glanced at Madison, Felix, and his sister. They nodded and looked absolutely confident in him. They'd follow him anywhere.

Even if that meant following him into certain danger . . . and maybe death.

There was no time to lose. They had to get out there and explore the crumbling remains of the human world before the Ch'zar came.

Ethan and Sterling Squadron had to find the Resistance a new home.

"Just one more thing," the colonel told Ethan.

She presented him a black carbon-fiber patch. It was the size of his palm and much like the patches they'd taught him to use to repair a flight suit.

Ethan turned it over. On the other side were crossed insect wings, a bundle of arrows underneath, all surrounded by a semicircle of gold stars. The insignia of a real Resister pilot!

Ethan's heart pounded wildly, and despite everything, he couldn't help but grin.

"With all the commotion, we forgot about these." Colonel Winter actually managed a slight smile back at Ethan. "You've earned your wings, Lieutenant Blackwood."

° ° ° ACKNOWLEDGMENTS ° ° °

Profound thanks to Syne and Kai, Diane Landolf, and Richard Curtis.

° ° ° **ABOUT THE AUTHOR** ° ° °

ERIC NYLUND is a *New York Times* bestselling and World Fantasy Award–nominated author. He is also director of narrative design for Microsoft Game Studios, where he helps create blockbuster video games.

Eric has bachelor's and master's degrees in chemistry. He graduated from the prestigious Clarion West Writers Workshop in 1994. He lives in the Pacific Northwest with his family. You can learn more about Eric and contact him at ericnylund.net.